"Good evening, Major," said a drawling, familiar voice. "Took you longer than I figured."

Mosby's hands dropped to the pistols at his hips, fell slowly away as the muzzle of a musket jammed into his spine. A ring of blue-clad Yankees materialized out of the night and formed a close ring about them.

"Take them to the stockade," said the lieutenant. "And double the guard. Can't take any chances on our prizes getting away — one of them Rebs is Mosby, the guerrilla."

"We're goin' to take real pleasure in seein' you hang, buster," added the burly sergeant. "We're goin' to put the show on right out in front of old Sam Grant. This is one order I figure he'll enjoy seeing carried out."

General Grant had issued an order calling for the hanging of any Ranger immediately upon capture, particularly John Mosby, one of the war's most feared and deadly leaders . . .

Rebel Ghost

REBEL GHOST

RAY HOGAN

PaperJacks LTD.

TORONTO   NEW YORK

PaperJacks

REBEL GHOST

PaperJacks LTD

330 STEELCASE RD. E., MARKHAM, ONT. L3R 2M1
210 FIFTH AVE., NEW YORK, N.Y. 10010

PaperJacks edition published November 1987

CAN ISBN 0-7701-0825-3
US ISBN 0-7701-0741-9
Printed in the USA

REBEL GHOST

Chapter One

The cannonball whistled as it passed overhead, thudded solidly into the earth when it struck. Hob Lovan twisted about, gazed thoughtfully at the plume of dust and litter that spewed upward.

"Six days this's been goin' on," he muttered. "Somethin's sure got to give soon."

John Mosby, Major, commander of the 43rd Battalion, Confederate Rangers, nodded. Almost a full week of pure hell. Days and nights of thundering guns, shattering explosions, shrilling horses, screaming men — and wholesale destruction. As the wizened old scout said, an end must come soon.

They were crouched behind a low ridge just west of Spottsylvania Court House. The fighting raged all around them in a broad half circle. Mosby had just lately rejoined Lee's Army of Northern Virginia, now stubbornly resisting U.S. Grant and his mighty Union force as it fought on in an avowed effort to occupy Richmond, a short fifty miles to the south, and end the war.

But the canny Lee had stalled the drive. He had

thrown up defenses around Spottsylvania, halted Grant dead in his tracks despite Yankee superiority in guns and number of men. Grant was taking it hard. He still smarted under the outmaneuvering he had received at the hands of the Confederate commander in the Battle of the Wilderness, and now his massive assaults on the heights around Spottsylvania were being thrown back time after time. But he was hanging on, determined as a bulldog.

A message sent by him to President Lincoln in Washington, and intercepted by Confederate agents, declared in part: ''I propose to fight it out on these lines if it takes all summer . . .''

And likely it would if he chose to continue his attempts to break through Lee's stubborn defenses. But John Mosby had his doubts that Grant would elect to pursue that route. Although the Union army outnumbered the Confederates by fifty thousand soldiers, Yankee losses in that May, 1864 campaign had been tremendous; so great in fact that Northern newspapers were asking questions and the ugly title of *Butcher* was being applied to the Union commander, who, just a few months previous, had been placed in charge of all Federal forces.

It was only common sense to believe Grant would change his tactics, attempt another course. Logically, he could fall back and endeavor to swing wide of Lee's entrenched forces. But such a movement had not been successful before. Lee had anticipated that very maneuver after the Wilderness engagement, had quickly withdrawn and met Grant head-on from a new position. What then could Grant do?

John Mosby felt himself considering the problem with no enthusiasm. Since his return he had become aware of a disinterest in the war's problems and activities other than that of simply doing what was expected of him. He was also aware of why these changes had come to be.

Jeb Stuart was dead. Stuart the magnificent, the bold, the reckless, the imaginative — who fired to the heights all men who came in contact with him — was dead. John Mosby was still having difficulty in accepting the fact and adjusting to it.

It had occurred shortly after the terrible struggle of the Wilderness. Mosby had been sent on a scouting mission by Lee. Stuart, with his cavalry, had been ordered to fall back toward Richmond and guard the approaches to the Confederate capital from any raids by Phil Sheridan and other Union detachments. There had been a sharp engagement at Yellow Tavern. Sheridan had been turned back, but a pistol bullet had felled the burly, red-bearded giant and the war was over for him.

The death of Stuart had been a grievous blow to Robert E. Lee and the Confederacy, but to John Mosby it was a personal tragedy. They had been close friends for years, had worked and fought through many campaigns together. Mosby's 43rd Battalion was a part of Stuart's cavalry and when word reached the Ranger chief of the officer's death, some of the daring-dash and glowing flame that had earned him his fame died also.

Now, John Mosby, the peerless Ranger, the scourge of the Union forces, the rebel ghost whom the northern armies would most like to capture — excepting of course, Robert E. Lee — wished for the war's end. The South must win, of course, but he hoped it would be soon. The glitter, the glamour, the sheer joy of fighting was gone. He wished mightily he could go home to his wife and their two small children and forget about death and devastation.

But the struggle was far from over. Early that day previous matters had turned critical for the Confederates. Hancock, under Grant's orders, had hurled his divisions at the right center of Lee's lines. He chose as his objective a salient occupied by southern General Edward Johnson. The position was forward of Lee's main entrenchments and Johnson had been directed to hold it at all costs; Union artillery, it was readily seen, could wreak havoc with southern defenses should it gain so advantageous a location.

Hancock overran Johnson. The general, along with brother officer G. H. Stewart and three thousand Confederate soldiers, was taken prisoner. Further, twenty-five field guns were captured and a serious breach in Lee's lines had been accomplished.

Hancock, flushed with success, had surged ahead. He had severed the Confederate ranks, was now in position to drive the disjointed wings apart. General J. B. Gordon, commanding Jubal Early's division, raced in to plug the gap. Rodes and Wilcox hurried to his assistance. They met the rampaging Hancock. The clash continued throughout most of the day but finally the Yankees faltered, fell back and the breach was healed.

Grant, meanwhile, taking advantage of the furious activity near the center of Lee's defenses, ordered attacks on the Confederate left and right wings. He presumed Lee had weakened those flanks to reinforce the center against Hancock's onslaughts. It was an error. The Grey Fox of the Confederacy had anticipated such a move on the part of the Federal leader and Generals Burnside and Warren were driven back in decisive defeat.

Grant then paused to recover his breath and consider. Lee, taking advantage of the Yankee's hesitancy, pulled his lines together tightly and reorganized. There was no recovering the salient lost to Hancock, or the men and equipment captured, but the consolidation meant strength and the Confederacy stood firm.

Mosby and his Rangers had been a part of it all. They had forsaken their usual scouting and raiding activities to reinforce Lee's stand as much as possible. Every available man was needed in the lines, Lee had said, and the Rangers had pitched in to do their share from hastily dug trenches and hurriedly built breastworks.

Had Stuart still been alive Mosby doubtless would have been with him riding with the cavalry, striking at and harassing the Union forces from every quarter. But Jeb Stuart was dead and in his place now rode Wade Hampton, an able man but one who lacked the flair of the spectacular Stuart.

Mosby had not been offered the command, as many thought he would be. He had not expected it. There were too many ranking officers entitled to fill the job. Mosby was thankful for one thing, however; the command had not gone to Fitzhugh-Lee as some had assumed. Fitzhugh-Lee, to the Ranger's way of thinking, was unsuited for the post, and for him to have taken over Jeb Stuart's cavalrymen would have been a mistake. Hampton had been a wise choice — but he was not Jeb Stuart.

Mosby knew he must shake off the lethargy that gripped him. He must carry on; it was expected of him not only by General Lee but by his own Rangers who respected him and looked to him for leadership. But he was finding it difficult to meet those obligations. War without Stuart was a monotonous grind, a humdrum, bitter affair.

He crouched lower behind the ridge as another cannonball screamed overhead. Somewhere a bugle was sounding a charge — a Yankee bugle from the location of it — and there was the steady racket of musket fire coming from the ravine to their right.

He saw a dozen or more blue-clad soldiers appear suddenly on the crest of a low rise, rush forward and pitch into a brushy hollow. He considered that for a moment, wondered if it could be only the activity of a small contingent or if it was the beginning of a new assault on the Confederate entrenchments.

He frowned, his lean, somewhat sharp face set to severe angles. Mosby was a small man but all bone, muscle and steel nerves. His hair was long and sandy-colored, and the beard he was permitting to grow was slightly reddish. He raised himself slightly, watched the gully more closely, endeavoring to make out what was taking place. He could see nothing. No more men appeared on the rise.

But the movement had some meaning. Of that he was sure. He should slip down, take a closer look. If it were a general movement forward by the Yankees, Lee must be advised of it quickly.

"Major . . ."

Mosby turned, faced a young soldier who had come up from behind him. "Yes?"

"The General would like to see you, sir. Said he'd appreciate it if you'd report to headquarters at once."

"All right, Corporal," Mosby replied, dismissing the messenger. He swung his attention back to the ravine. There were still no signs of the Yankees but he felt the situation should be watched. He motioned to Hob Lovan. The bushy-browed, bearded old scout wormed his way closer.

"Something going on down there in that pocket," the Ranger chief said. "Keep an eye on it."

Lovan cocked his head, studied Mosby. "What you figurin' to do, crawl down there for a look-see? If so, I'm goin' along. Let somebody else do the watchin'."

Mosby said, "No, not that. The General sent for me."

Lovan settled back, satisfied. "All right, Major, I'll watch sharp. But if the Gen'ral's got somethin' special for us to do, count me in. This here wallerin' around like a bunch of groundhogs in a hole is chawin' my nerves."

"Know just what you mean," Mosby said sympathetically and pulled back from the ridge.

Chapter Two

He hoped Lee did have a mission for him to undertake, preferably one of dangerous proportions. Such would take his mind off Stuart's death and put him back in touch with reality again. But he had doubts. Lee was pulling in every soldier available to man the defenses. He would not wish to spare anyone.

Mosby made his way toward the rear in long, hurried strides. A momentary lull had come in the fighting and men were sprawled about everywhere, some working on their weapons, others catching a few winks of hard-earned sleep. That most were near total exhaustion was apparent. Grant's superiority in numbers was beginning to tell. Where he had the reserves to throw fresh troops continually into the assault, Lee was compelled to call upon the same battle-weary veterans time after time.

He reached the hut that had been commandeered for Lee's field quarters and entered. He found the southern leader waiting with a half dozen of his officers. Lee appeared worn and haggard. His hair was a white halo about his head and his eyes showed a deep sadness. But he smiled when he saw Mosby.

"Thank you for coming promptly, Major," he said in that soft, unhurried way of his. "Please be seated."

Mosby took an empty chair at the table, nodding at the others — the balding Ewell, square-shouldered J. B. Gordon; Rodes, wearing no beard but with a full, sweeping mustache; the huge Jubal Early; A. P. Hill; the wounded Walker, and several more. The one civilian present was Jasper Denning, the sutler who served Lee also as a sort of unofficial secret agent.

The room was thick with cigar smoke, warm from the late spring weather. All but Lee and Gordon had unbuttoned their coats, had them open at the collar or entirely down the front. It was the first staff meeting Mosby had been summoned to attend since his return and not to see the broad, friendly face of Jeb Stuart among those present drove home again the extent of his personal loss.

"Major," Lee said, spreading his hands flat on the table, "we again have need of your exceptional talents."

"I am at your service, sir," Mosby replied quietly. He felt a quickening of his pulse. It was to be a mission after all.

"As you can well realize we are in desperate straits," Lee continued. "I will not attempt to hide such from you, or any man in the service of the Confederate army. We have halted General Grant, yes, but it can be only temporary. We cannot hold out for long.

"We are greatly outnumbered in both men and

ordnance. It is a tribute to every southern soldier that we have done as well as we have. With the odds two to one against us, we have thrown them back. But now matters are critical.''

"That's the God's truth," Hill muttered feelingly. "If any more of our positions are overrun, as was Johnson's, we're in a bad way.''

"The attack seems to have slackened," Mosby said. "At least in the sector where I've been.''

"True, but I mistrust that," Lee said, rising. "I believe that to be a part of Grant's strategy. Mr. Denning here," he added, waving at the sutler, "has brought me information that was picked up by one of his associates only this morning. We are indebted to him again for the fine service he has rendered us.''

Mosby glanced at the sutler. He was a tall, wiry man, dark-faced and dark-haired. He was clean shaven and generally managed to look well dressed and neatly groomed despite the elementary conditions the southern soldiers continually bucked. He had strung along with the Army of Northern Virginia since Gettysburg, maintaining his three supply wagons with the help of two partners, Hugo Bishop and Oliver Moon.

Denning and his associates were not particularly liked by men in the ranks since they insisted on doing business on a strictly cash basis. But they served a need for those who were able to scrape up money with which to make purchases. And, as Lee had mentioned, Denning and his partners had been of assistance in picking up and passing on information pertaining to the Union army that often was of value.

"Grant plans to withdraw," Lee said, beginning to pace slowly back and forth. His face was tipped down, his hands clasped behind him. "Failing to dislodge us from this point, he now intends to swing around us, drive for Richmond on a direct line. His losses here have been monstrous. There is rumor that Washington is far from satisfied with his efforts."

Jubal Early stirred, voiced the question that sprang to Mosby's lips.

"Do we know this to be a fact, General? Grant tried to bypass us before, after the Wilderness. Seems improbable he would attempt the maneuver again."

"We have this information from Mr. Denning. He assures me his source is absolutely reliable. And it makes good sense. While we are successful each time in halting an assault on our forces, we nevertheless eventually must fall back to protect our capital. Thus Grant actually makes a gain."

"We win the battle but are losing the war," Rodes observed succinctly.

"A precise statement of fact," Lee said. "And a truth we must accept whether we wish to or not."

There was a long pause. Outside the small structure cannon boomed dully, and somewhere a brisk encounter between musketmen was taking place. But the fighting was sporadic and desultory.

"Then your decision is to abandon our position here and fall back toward Richmond?" Gordon asked, finally.

"I see no other recourse," Lee replied. He looked again at Jasper Denning. "You will kindly repeat what you have told me, sir."

The sutler removed the cigar from his lips. He pushed his wide-brimmed planter's hat to the back of his head, leaned forward on his elbows.

"Grant's plan," he said, "is to pull off. He will circle out to do his best to sweep in behind you. This likely means a forced march to Milford, or some point near that settlement. Then, standing between you and Richmond, he will be sending occupying troops into the capital while he fends off your main force with the greater part of his own army."

Again there was a silence. Early cleared his throat. "He's got the men to do it, too," he said. "Won't take but a couple of regiments to occupy Richmond."

"Exactly," Lee said, still pacing restlessly. "It leaves only one door open to us. We must immediately withdraw, beat him to the North Anna River, and be waiting for him just as we were here at Spottsylvania. We cannot permit him to get between us and the capital."

"The North Anna would be a good place to make a stand," Ewell said, drumming on the table lightly with his fingers. "But, outnumbered as we are — two to one as you say — I'm not certain we can hold . . ."

"We have no choice, General," Lee broke in gently. He swung his solemn face to Mosby. "That is where you come in, Major. We need every available soldier if we are to save Richmond. And to that purpose, I want you to get a message through to General Breckinridge."

Chapter Three

Breckinridge!

Interest stirred within John Mosby. Breckinridge was far away — somewhere in the Shenandoah Valley. Getting to him would be no simple task; a hundred thousand or more Yankees barred the route.

"Then all our communication lines must be down," Rodes said, his voice strained.

"Yes, even those to Lynchburg," Lee replied.

Rodes wagged his head. "I had no idea it was that bad."

"It is worse than bad, if such is possible," Lee said quietly. He turned to the Ranger. "It will be necessary that you find General Breckinridge. His exact position is unknown, but at last report he was near the town of New Market. He was expecting to engage General Sigel's forces in that area. If he has done so and was successful, you will doubtless find him farther north. If the opposite is true, he will have retired southward, or to the west."

Mosby nodded. "I understand. When he is located what do I tell him?"

"Advise him that he is to abandon his activities in the Shenandoah and hasten to join us at the North Anna River. We must have his brigades."

"What about Pickett and Hoke?" Early suggested. "They are at full strength. Why not pull them in, too?"

"I am taking measures to do just that," Lee said. "But there is no problem in contacting them such as exists with General Breckinridge. I assume you are aware of that problem, Major?"

Mosby said, "Yes, sir. As matters stand, the only route to the Shenandoah is straight through the Union army."

"Correct. There is neither time nor an alternative way available that permits otherwise. I realize that it is asking much of you, Major, but we must have Breckinridge's support."

"Breck will have the devil's own time getting to us," Rodes commented. "Lot of Yankees between the Shenandoah and the North Anna."

"You will make the general aware of that fact," Lee said, pausing beside Mosby. "It would be my suggestion that he follow the valley turnpike to Piedmont — assuming he is still in the vicinity of New Market — and swing east to the river from that point. He should stay on the south bank, of course."

"What about Sigel?" Jubal Early asked. "Do we just leave the Shenandoah to him?"

It was a full minute before the Commander of the Confederate armies replied. Then, "I regret that there is nothing else to be done. We can only hope that General Jones, with his small force, can employ it effectively. He can be no match for Sigel in an all-out engagement, but perhaps he will take a leaf from the book of Major Mosby and his Rangers and occupy his time with harassing and delaying activities.''

"About all he can do," Gordon said. "Shame we must abandon the Shenandoah," he added, as an afterthought.

"A loss I will admit," Lee replied, "but we must look at it from the overall standpoint." He came back again to Mosby. "Major, do you have any questions?''

"How much time do I have to get the message through?''

"We shall start to withdraw tomorrow, the fourteenth. We could possibly delay until the fifteenth, depending upon Grant. If General Breckinridge can get started by the sixteenth and encounters no serious delays he should be able to join us before the Union army can get into position. But time is critical. Please impress that upon the general.''

"Yes, sir.''

"Are you acquainted with him or do you wish a written dispatch bearing his instructions?''

"I know the general very well. He will take my word.''

"Good. Now, Major, how soon can you leave?''

Mosby shrugged. "Tonight. As soon as it is dark, anyway.''

"Excellent. Feel free to requisition the quartermaster for whatever you need. How many Rangers will you take with you?''

"Only one.''

Gordon looked up in surprise. "One? Won't that be stretching it too thin, John? Take along several men — then one of you is bound to get through.''

"Works both ways," the Ranger said. "With just two of us the risk of detection is considerably decreased.''

"Of course," the Confederate leader said. "Never thought of it that way.''

Lee moved to his chair and sat down, a lean, gaunt man sagging under the weight of command. He lifted his eyes to the Ranger chief, studied him thoughtfully for a moment.

In a low voice he said, "John, I've seen you accept my assignments with a great deal more enthusiasm than you have displayed here today. Is it that you have doubts as to the outcome?''

Mosby shifted on his chair, shook his head. "I can't explain it . . . But don't worry about me getting through . . .''

"Jeb Stuart's death has affected us all," Lee cut in softly, kindly, putting his finger on the problem instantly. "But we must not permit it to change our values, alter our determination to do our duties as we see them. Jeb would be the first to say that. Keep that in mind.''

Mosby said, "Of course, sir. And thank you for reminding me of it.''

Lee extended his hand across the table. "Good luck, Major. Our prayers go with you.''

Mosby took his commander's slender fingers into his own and pressed them firmly. "And mine with you. We'll find Breckinridge, never fear.''

"If it can be done, I am certain you will," Lee said. "But I cannot help consider the terrible risk.''

"Something we all share as long as this war goes on," Mosby replied and rose to his feet.

He shook hands with the others. When he came to Jubal Early the officer said, "Tell Breck for me that we need him bad — to not spare the horses getting to the North Anna."

"I'll do that," Mosby said, smiling, and wheeled toward the door. Jasper Denning, standing close by the exit, offered his hand.

"Let me wish you well, Major. You have a difficult job ahead of you."

Mosby accepted the sutler's best wishes in silence. He had never been particularly friendly with Denning, mostly because he had little regard for any man who turned his efforts to making profit from soldiers involved in fighting a war for their country.

"Do I understand you plan to leave as quickly as it is dark?" Denning continued.

The Ranger thought for a moment, pondering the question. "Before morning, at any rate. Why?"

The sutler shrugged his shoulders. "No reason. Just a matter of curiosity. I thought you might want to take time and check my wagons for items you might need."

Mosby moved on toward the door. "I'm obliged to you, but I believe I have everything necessary."

He stepped out into the fading sunlight. Denning's two partners, Moon and Bishop, lounged against a shed directly opposite the house. They smiled, nodded to him as he passed. He gave them only slight notice, his mind now dwelling on the task that lay ahead.

One man — he had told Lee that was all he would require for the job. He would take Hob Lovan. The old scout would be a perfect choice.

He knew the country well, especially the Shenandoah area, and when it came to slipping through the hills and valleys unseen and unheard, he had no equal.

Mosby swung back toward the lines, striking for the ridge where he had left the scout. Lovan had asked to go on any mission that Lee had in mind; he would be pleased that he was chosen. The scout was still watching the ravine when Mosby wormed his way to his side.

"Ain't seen no Yanks down there yet," he said as the Ranger chief settled down beside him. "Could be they're a-tunnelin' under."

Mosby grinned at the dry humor. "If they are, we won't be here to welcome them."

Hob's leathery face lit up. "We goin' somewheres?"

"To find Breckinridge — over in the Shenandoah."

The scout whistled softly. "Well, I'll say this for the Gen'ral, he sure don't pick puny chores for us! Who all's goin' and when do we start?"

"Just the two of us, and just as soon after sundown as we can get away."

"Sounds like we might be in a hurry. What's it all about?"

Mosby went into details on the mission, putting particular emphasis on the absolute necessity for at least one of them getting through to Breckinridge with Lee's orders. When he was finished Lovan stared thoughtfully out across the smoky, torn hills.

"Well, I expect we'll get the job done sure enough, Major. What bothers me is you."

"Me?" Mosby exclaimed. "Why?"

"Well, if I can do my talkin' like a friend, you just ain't yourself no more. Was we to get a little chore like this a month ago, you'd a been all hepped up over it. You'd a been a-rarin' to go, and figurin' out ways to aggravate the Yankees every step. Now . . ."

"Now?" Mosby pressed softly, urging Lovan to complete his words.

"Now you act like it was somethin' you had to do," the scout finished in a quick rush. "You ain't got no more spirit for it than a kid startin' his first day at school! There somethin' weightin' down your mind, Major?"

John Mosby studied the backs of his hands. He was remembering what Lee had said back in his quarters, realizing again the truth of his words. He reached out, laid a hand on Lovan's shoulder.

"I'll be all right, Hob. Guess I've been doing a bit too much thinking lately."

He glanced toward the west. It would be dark in another three hours, and he wanted to be on the move shortly thereafter. There would be no delaying until morning, as he had implied to Jasper Denning. That had been merely a reply to satisfy the sutler. He had learned long ago to always keep his exact plans to himself.

"Let's pull out of here and get ready to leave," he said. "Few things that have to be done first."

Hob Lovan rolled to his back. "Personally," he said, looking around at the pits and trenches with obvious distaste, "I'm ready to take off right now. You just say the word."

Mosby smiled again. "Dark — that will be soon enough," he replied.

Chapter Four

It was shortly after nine o'clock when John Mosby and Hob Lovan slipped quietly out of the Confederate encampment.

The Ranger chief had left behind the cape and plumed hat he generally wore, was dressed now in black boots, gray breeches and dark shirt. His weapons consisted of the two revolvers carried on his hips and a knife worn inside his right boot, a custom all Rangers were taught to observe.

The scout's equipment was much the same with the exception of his footgear. He preferred soft-soled moccasin-type shoes similar to those worn by Indians. On his head he had a knitted skullcap. They left their horses behind. It would be much easier to work their way through the Union lines without mounts — and when the need arose there would be plenty of Yankee horses available.

Mosby had left the balance of the Rangers in the command of Jess Hilliard, a capable young lieutenant who hailed from one of the Carolinas. He had considered at some length to whom the responsibility should be relegated during his absense and finally decided on Hilliard. For the first time in the war the 43rd Battalion was fighting as a stationary unit from a specific position, and he realized it would require a firm hand and a cool head to keep his usually far-ranging soldiers under control.

The Rangers, ordinarily, operated in a manner vastly different from the average battalion. They were all selected men, chosen by Mosby personally and taught by him the art of guerrilla warfare. They observed no strict camp routine, did no marching or drilling, spent their time instead becoming expert horsemen and ultra proficient in harassing tactics, the wrecking of railroads, destroying wagon trains and in performing scout and courier duties.

They were likened to ghosts wheeling through the forests and valleys, friends to all who sympathized with the South, a bane to their enemies. Their reputation spread throughout the country and Grant had found them so troublesome that he issued an order calling for the hanging of any Ranger, particularly John Mosby, immediately upon capture. But, except in one or two instances, the directive had gone begging. Few Yankees were ever offered the opportunity of carrying it out for Mosby and his Rangers were elusive shadows, here one moment, seemingly miles away the next.

It was a reckless, romantic way of fighting a war and membership in the 43rd was eagerly sought. For one thing it permitted a man to carry on his usual mode of life. During the time when he was not needed to participate in a raid or go on a mission, a Ranger was allowed to return to his home. There he pursued his profession or vocation, even his closest friends and sometimes his relatives unaware that he was a member of the feared Rangers. Listed on the roster could be found farmers, clerks, mine and mill employees, even physicians and lawyers. At the outbreak of the struggle, John Mosby himself had been a lawyer.

He had been living in Bristol at that time and was enjoying a good practice. When the political issues became apparent he had taken a stand for the preservation of the Union, agreeing with Abraham Lincoln on that point. But States Rights had been a different matter and when his native Virginia seceded, he felt his loyalties lay there, and he joined with the others in the formation of the Confederate army.

He had enlisted under Jeb Stuart and rose rapidly through the ranks. Stuart, recognizing his abilities, had used him as a scout on many occasions and eventually permitted him to form his band of Rangers. It was a strange paradox that the mild, bookish lawyer who could quote Bryant's poetry with offhand ease should emerge as one of the war's most feared and deadly leaders.

Under Jeb Stuart Mosby had taken great pride in his battalion. He had striven hard to make the 43rd an effective group respected by all. And then with the death of the cavalry general, his interest sagged. The war appeared as it really was, a terrible, bloody, wearisome affair with its ultimate purpose obscured in a mist of frustration and grief.

But now, creeping silently through the brush with Hob Lovan, John Mosby was feeling again the pound of excitement, the hard, pulsing pressure of danger he loved so well. It was all flowing back into him and he was realizing the simple, lonely truth that had not appeared to him before; the war continued — and the living must take up where the dead left off, otherwise it all was in vain.

"Major . . ." Lovan whispered softly. "Sentries ahead."

Mosby came to a halt. He stared through the filmy darkness. Two Union soldiers, muskets on their shoulders, stood at the edge of a clearing ten yards distant. They had reached the Yankee line. Once they got beyond the sentries they would be within the Union encampment. Extreme care would be doubly necessary then for they would be entirely surrounded by enemy soldiers and the slightest misstep would mean disaster.

"We take 'em, Major?"

Mosby shook his head. "Can't risk a disturbance."

In the dead silence of the night he studied the two Yankees. Behind them, only a yard or two, was a low, stone wall, evidently a property boundary. Apparently the army was using it as a natural marker for camp limits. To their left would be the pits and trenches that had been dug, the breastworks and other defenses that had been erected. There should be more of the same to the right, Mosby reasoned. From that he would guess they were somewhere in between, near full center.

"We'll try going around them," Mosby said then in a whisper. "But don't swing too wide. May be others all through here. If we run into trouble, use your knife."

Lovan nodded. He drew his knife, placed the blade between his teeth. Dropping to his hands and knees, he started off to the right, silent as a breeze brushing through a field of wheat. Mosby was beside him and together they worked in closer to the guards.

The night was still. The guns had ceased and, strangely, there were none of the camp sounds normally audible; no laughing, no occasional shout or solitary singing . . . Nothing . . . The Yankees evidently were as exhausted by the struggle that was taking place as were the Confederates.

They crept in nearer the sentries. A faint, metallic click off to their right drew Mosby up sharply. He glanced that way, saw two more pickets. They were not more than fifty feet distant. The Yankees had a tight ring around their encampment. It had been no great problem picking a route through the trenches and breastworks but it appeared it would not be so simple getting into the camp itself.

Mosby touched Lovan lightly on the shoulder and they sank back into the brush. It would not be possible to fool the sentries by tossing a rock to one side and drawing their attention. The other guards would also be attracted by the sound, thus voiding the hope of sprinting across the open ground that lay between.

The scout turned to Mosby. ''Crossin' over's goin' to be ticklish. You got any ideas?''

''Could try the old trick of covering up with brush and crawling. Dark enough.''

''Unless one of them Yanks recollected there weren't no brush growin' out there in the first place.''

''Would take too much time, anyway.''

"I'd say our chances was just about as good as any was we to jump up and run for it. Ain't far across to that wall."

"They'd drop us with a musket ball before we got half way. And even if they missed, they'd rouse the whole camp."

Which was a situation they must avoid at all costs, Mosby knew. He looked up suddenly. "Does give me an idea," he said. "Grab yourself a stone — like this one." The Ranger leader picked up a rock the size of his fist. "When I give you the word, you throw yours off into the brush beyond the pickets to the right. I'll do the same on the left. With luck they'll be looking in opposite directions . . ."

"While we're makin' a run for it," Lovan finished. "Ought to work."

"When the rocks hit the ground, that's when we go. Ready?"

"Ready."

Mosby set himself for a quick dash across the clearing. He glanced at Lovan. The scout was crouched, poised to run.

"Now," he murmured.

The stones fell at almost identical seconds into the brush on either side. There was a clatter and dry rattle. At the initial sound Mosby saw the guards nearest him wheel and come to sudden attention, their faces turned toward the disturbance. Instantly he was up and away, running swiftly and silently. There was no time to see if Hob Lovan was with him. The scout would look out for himself, the one thought in his mind also being to gain the shelter of the darkness beyond the wall.

Mosby went over the stone hedge in a low dive,

coming down into the brush. Lovan was on his heels, landing almost on top of him. There was a sharp crackling as branches and twigs crushed beneath their weight.

"What was that?" The picket's voice was filled with alarm.

"Don't know . . . Was over there by the wall . . ."

"Let's have a look."

Mosby gathered his feet under him. "Come on," he hissed to Lovan and hurried off into the night.

They ran hard for a long fifty yards, keeping low and well within the shadows. They could hear the sentries back along the wall, beating through the bushes, clambering about the rocks. The Yankees seemed to be concentrating their efforts in that one area.

"Prob'ly figured us for varmints of some kind," the scout said when they paused for breath.

Mosby, sucking deep for wind, nodded. "Let's hope they keep on thinking it."

They remained beneath the tangle of brush and vines for a full five minutes. Finally, all was quiet again and Mosby, rising, looked ahead.

"Know about where we are?" Lovan asked.

"On the edge of the camp," the Ranger chief replied. "We're behind Yankee lines now."

"And we're goin' right straight through the middle, that it?"

"No other way. We've got to get to the far side, to the road that runs to Germanna Ford. We make it to that point we can hunt up some horses."

Lovan cocked his eyes to the heavens. "Gettin' later every minute. Reckon we ought to be movin'.

Ain't goin' to be no place for the likes of us, come daylight.''

They struck off into the wood, walking in long, easy strides that covered the ground fast. A hundred yards farther in they caught a glimpse of white tents through the trees. Watch fires began to spot the darkness.

Mosby knew there was no possibility of circling wide in the hope of avoiding the camp. It was much too extensive. Their best bet, and likely the safest, was to cut through the center, past the tents with their weary, slumbering soldiers, and gain the opposite edge. It should actually be easier as they worked deeper into the Union camp, Mosby reasoned. There would be fewer guards.

They came to the first row of canvas shelters, paused in the deep brush behind them. A lone picket stood watch fifty feet away, back to them, head dropped forward on his chest. Motioning to Lovan for caution, Mosby skirted the dozing sentry and moved on.

They forged ahead, going sometimes behind a line of tents, other times being forced to walk boldly between twin rows. They saw few guards for it was as Mosby had expected; the nearer they got to the heart of the bivouac, the lesser the precautions. Apparently the Yankees feared little from the northern side of their encampment, and concentrated their safeguards to the south.

They reached what appeared to be the center of operations, judging from the number of crude and hastily constructed buildings that were gathered in a fair sized clearing. These would be headquarters for Grant and his officers, along with field hospitals, kitchens and supply depots. There was considerable activity here and the Rangers swung wide, taking no chances.

Beyond that they were again moving between rows of tents, finding it absurdly easy to slip by the few sentries watching over the sleeping soldiers, until finally the lines of white pyramids ended and they found themselves at the edge of a well traveled road. Mosby drew to a halt in the brush along its shoulder.

"This goes to Germanna Ford," he said in a low voice. "Keep your eyes peeled from here on for horses."

"Been watchin' but I ain't seen a horse for an hour. Stables must be on the other side of the camp."

"Probably," Mosby replied. "Can you think of any other place around here where we can cross the Rapidan except at Germanna Ford?"

The scout removed his skullcap, scratched at his thinning hair. "Nope, not this time of year, unless you're figurin' to swim. You ain't likin' the idea of Germanna?"

The ranger shook his head. "It's the one point where we could run into trouble. Bound to be sentries there."

"Ain't had no trouble with them yet."

"It will be different at the ford."

They resumed the march, following the course of the road but staying in the brush that grew along its edges. An hour later Mosby again halted. Lovan moved up to his shoulder.

"Somethin' wrong?"

"Horses," Mosby replied, pointing to a soft blur in the darkness ahead. "Looks like a cavalry patrol bedded down for the night."

"Just what we're lookin' for!" the scout chortled happily. "And we ain't far from the crossin'."

"A mile, maybe less."

"Couldn't have worked out better. I'm sure gettin' tired of this walkin'."

Mosby nodded his agreement. The cavalry was likely stationed at the ford, its duty being to watch over all who crossed the river. It was a fortunate break, Mosby thought. It should be simple to obtain two of the horses, lead them quietly to the Rapidan and escape into the night. They could expect at least one sentry at the ford, perhaps even two, but they should present no serious difficulty.

He repeated his thoughts to the scout. Lovan wagged his head. "Be easy as skinnin' a cat," he said.

There was no sentry standing guard over the dozen or so animals. All were tethered to a picket rope that had been strung taut between two trees. They were saddled and bridled, attesting to the fact the Yankees kept them in readiness for instant use.

Mosby and Lovan crept in, choosing the two horses at the end farthest from the mounds of blankets scattered about in a small clearing a few yards away. Mosby halted beside the animal he would take, reached for the short rope that linked it to the tight line. He gave it a tug. It failed to pull free as it should.

He glanced at Lovan. The scout had encountered the same difficulty. A faint alarm arose within the Ranger. Soldiers leaving their mounts ready for quick, emergency use, would have tied them with the usual slip-knot which would permit instant release. He started to turn, to whisper a warning to Lovan, when a drawling voice, vaguely familiar, came suddenly from the shadows beyond the horses.

"Good evening, Major."

Mosby's hands dropped to the pistols at his hips, fell slowly away as the muzzle of a musket jammed into his spine. A ring of blue-clad Yankees materialized out of the night and formed a close ring about Lovan and him.

"Took you longer than I figured, Major," the voice said. "Expected you at least two hours ago . . . Now, if you will kindly raise your hands . . ."

Mosby lifted his arms, eyes on the tall figure emerging from the darkness. A sharp breath escaped his lips. It was Jasper Denning, the sutler.

Chapter Five

Only it was Lieutenant Jasper Denning now.

Hob Lovan surveyed the Yankee uniform, spat in disgust. "A bluebelly! A damn traitorin' bluebelly!"

Denning halted near the old scout, favored him with a scornful look. "A Union officer — and proud of it. But no traitor. I'm a member of the army secret service and have been for two years."

Mosby felt his anger rise swiftly. "All the time you were with us — with General Lee — you were working for the Yankees!"

"Exactly, Major, and it has proved to be an effective system. I was always in position to know what was going on in the Confederate army and at the same time I could feed Lee the information we wanted him to have."

"And this story about Grant withdrawing . . ."

"It's true. And we don't mind General Lee knowing it. What difference will it make? End of the war is just a matter of time. A few months and the Army of Northern Virginia will be no more.

We just have to go through the motions of pushing it back to Richmond.''

''You're sort of countin' your cotton bales before the pickin's done, ain't you?'' Hob Lovan observed drily.

''Hardly,'' Denning replied. ''Simple arithmetic. Grant's forces are growing as he calls in his different corps. Time we're ready to move on Richmond we'll have well over a hundred and fifty thousand men. Lee will be lucky to muster half that number — even if he manages somehow to get word to Breckinridge and the others, which isn't likely now. Disarm these men, Sergeant.''

Mosby let his glance slide over the circle of Yankee cavalrymen. Fourteen in all. He remained silent while a burly non-com moved up beside him, removed his belt and pistols, also relieved Lovan of his weapon, and stepped back. He caught the scout's eyes, shook his head. To attempt a break at that moment would be sheer suicide. They must find a way of escape but it was only common sense to bide their time until there was at least a small chance of success.

''You thinking of making a run for it, Major?'' Denning asked, a half smile on his thin lips. ''I'd advise against it. While we have other plans for you, these men would still shoot you down before you got ten feet. It took considerable planning on my part to set up this little trap and you can be assured I have covered every possibility.''

''You planned this?'' Lovan exclaimed.

''Down to the last step. I — that is, Moon, Bishop and I left Lee's camp ahead of you. It had all been worked out beforehand. This is no chance meeting. We knew you would need horses and that you would cross the river at Germanna Ford. Thus it was easy to rig our snare.''

Mosby shook his head in apparent resignation. ''Looks like you've got us cold. But why? If it's not important that General Lee gets reinforcements, why go to all the bother of stopping us?''

''For you, Major,'' Denning said with a flourish of his hand. ''It's strictly in your honor. You are a bit of unfinished business the secret service assigned me to clear up. It appears I've been successful.''

''And we're goin' to take real pleasure in seein' you hang, buster,'' the burly sergeant added with a laugh. ''We're goin' to put the show on right out in front of old Sam Grant and all his big brass. This is one order I figure he'll enjoy seeing carried out.''

Mosby felt a chill slip through him. He could expect mercy from no one, particularly Grant. The Union commander considered him a guerrilla and outlaw despite the official recognition given him and the 43rd Battalion by the Confederate Congress and President Jefferson Davis. They enjoyed the same status as any regiment or division in the army but Grant chose to ignore that fact.

''You don't have much to say, Major,'' Denning said in a faintly sarcastic tone. ''You — the clever tactician who took such pride in plaguing the Union soldiers — who was always too high and mighty to associate with a common sutler . . .''

''Words aren't of much use now,'' Mosby said quietly. ''What comes next?''

''Next? Well, putting you two in a safe place until morning, that's what happens next. If General

Grant weren't here I'd hang you right now, but since he is, I think he's entitled to see the finish of the rebel army's chief guerrilla!''

Mosby stirred angrily. It always irked him to have the term guerrilla applied to the Rangers and himself. But he said nothing, merely waited.

Denning motioned at the non-com. ''Sergeant Neill, take them to the stockade. And double the guard for the balance of the night. Can't take any chances on our prizes getting away.''

Neill pushed forward, carrying a small coil of rope. He reached for Mosby's shoulder, spun the Confederate officer roughly about.

''Stick out your hands, Reb.''

Mosby did as directed. When his wrists were bound together tightly, he watched as Hob Lovan was accorded the same treatment.

''Now march,'' Neill barked. ''And walk slow. You men, mount up!'' he added to the cavalry-men. ''Fall in behind. First one of these Secesh to make a false move, lay your musket barrel across his head — but no shootin'. We want them alive for hangin'.''

Mosby, shoved hard by the sergeant, stumbled, recovered himself and began to walk along the road he and Lovan had just traveled. The scout came up beside him. Evidently they were being taken to the cluster of buildings he had assumed were Union headquarters. He had not noticed a stockade but it would be there, somewhere.

He cast a glance at Lovan, trudging silently along through the gloom. He knew the scout would not be giving up. He, too, would be thinking of their chances for escape, searching his mind for an idea that would enable them to cheat the Yankee gallows and complete their mission to Breckinridge.

He twisted, looked back over his shoulder. Neill and his cavalrymen, in the saddle, were crowded about him and Lovan in a tight half circle. Jasper Denning, with two other men, probably Moon and Bishop, were a few paces farther on. To attempt a break at that moment was out of the question.

"That Denning!" Lovan muttered. "That low livin', sneakin', lyin' bluebelly skunk! Never did have no use for him. Now I reckon I know why!"

"Quiet down there!" The Yankee sergeant snapped. "Be no talkin' . . ."

"I'll talk 'til I'm hung if it pleasures me!" Lovan shot back. "And no damn Yankee's goin' to . . ."

Neill spurred forward. He drew his saber, brought it down solidly, flat side up, across the old scout's shoulders. Hob staggered, went to his knees from the blow.

Mosby stooped quickly, helped the scout to his feet as best he could. He peered into Lovan's pain-twisted face, saw that he was not seriously injured. He spun to Neill.

"You're a brave man, Sergeant," he said coldly. "A credit to the uniform you're wearing."

The non-com swore, surged toward Mosby. The Confederate leader stood motionless, refused to give ground. Jasper Denning's voice cracked through the night.

"Sergeant!"

Neill jerked his horse to a stop. He glared at Mosby. "Damn you!" He ground the words out savagely. "I'd like to cleave you right down the middle — and I will if you give me cause! Got a personal score to settle with you! Some of your thievin' bunch murdered my brother . . .''

"Sergeant Neill! What's going on here?"

The cavalryman pulled his horse about, his face flushed and angry. "Nothin's wrong, sir. Just one of the prisoners actin' up."

Denning studied the non-com thoughtfully for a long minute, then transferred his gaze to Mosby. "We'll have no private matters settled here, Sergeant," he said crisply. "You know what I want done. You have your orders and I want them carried out to the letter. Understand?"

"Yes, sir, Lieutenant. It'll be as you say."

"All right. Now see to it."

Neill saluted stiffly and wheeled back into line with the others. Denning pulled away and rejoined his two companions. The sergeant waited until the officer was beyond earshot and then leaned toward Mosby.

"Get walkin', Reb," he said softly. "And I'm hopin' you take a notion to try somethin'. Far as I'm concerned, hangin' is too good for you. I'd like to take care of you myself — in my own way."

John Mosby smiled. "Just keep hoping, Sergeant," he said coolly, "and maybe you'll get your chance."

Chapter Six

The prison stockade appeared to be a barn from which all interior partitions had been removed, thus creating a large, hollow shell. The windows had been boarded up and the wide, double doors removed. Encircling it was a fence of ten foot high poles, sharpened at the tips and further reinforced by wire, strips of metal roofing and other miscellaneous materials.

It stood off to the left of the several buildings, on a low hill, and as they approached Mosby's sharp eyes sought out the guards and swiftly recorded other details that might lead to an avenue of escape. There were four sentries, he noted, one at each corner. There was but a single entrance, and that facing the camp.

They came to a halt before the gate. Immediately a soldier emerged from a small sentry hut some distance in front of the stockade, and trotted toward them. He produced a key, inserted it in a padlock that linked together a heavy chain that secured the gate. The log panel creaked open and he stepped back.

"More customers, eh, Sarge?"

Neill growled something unintelligible, jerked his head curtly at the Rangers. "Inside, Rebs."

Mosby and Lovan walked into the dark and silent compound. The gate closed on dry, squealing hinges. The chain rattled briefly and then they heard the snap of the lock.

"I'm assignin' four more men to guard duty here," Neill's voice said from the opposite side of the wall.

"Four? Why? What's up?"

"One of them Rebs we just brought in is Mosby, the guerrilla."

"Mosby!"

"Yeh. Ain't takin' no chances on him breakin' out. The lieutenant's figurin' on a hangin', come the mornin'."

"Mosby!" the sentry said in an awed sort of way. "That'll sure be a fine sight for old Sam, seein' him swingin' in the breeze. Who nabbed him, Amos, you?"

There was a pause and then Neill said, "Well, I reckon you can say I was in on the catch, sure enough. Of course the . . ."

"Everything all right here, Sergeant?"

It was Jasper Denning, dropping by for a final check.

"All set, sir," Neill replied. "We got 'em locked up and I'm sendin' over four extra guards. That'll make eight all told, plus Private Hopson here. There won't be nobody gettin' outside that stockade this night!"

"Fine. Now, you report to me first thing in the

morning. I'll go over your orders for the day then."

"Yes, sir, Lieutenant — good night . . ."

Conversation and other sounds beyond the fence died out. Mosby and Hob Lovan moved forward slowly, going deeper into the stockade. Men lay everywhere along the wall, all sleeping. Evidently the barn was filled and the overflow was spilling into the yard.

"Sure quite a passel of our boys here," Lovan remarked. "Must be two-three hundred at least."

"At least," the Ranger agreed. "Possibly more."

They reached the gaping doorway and halted. It was completely dark under the roof but it required only a quick glance to see that the area was packed.

"I been tryin' to figure a way . . ." Lovan began and broke off abruptly as Mosby lifted a hand in warning.

A man had detached himself from the depths of the barn, was coming toward them. He stepped over the sleeping prisoners carefully, pausing once to retrieve a fallen cap and replace it gently on the owner's head. He halted before the two Rangers.

"Welcome to the Kirkwood House, gentlemen," he said in ironic humor. "Accommodations are a bit crowded but we can always make room for more. Who . . ."

The speaker was a young captain. He still wore most of his uniform and there was a bandage around his left hand. He leaned forward, looked more closely into the Confederate officer's face. He drew back suddenly.

"Major Mosby!" he exclaimed in surprise. "It is, isn't it?"

"Right, Captain. My partner here is Hob Lovan, also of the 43rd Battalion. I think I've seen you before. With General Johnson's troops, weren't you?"

"Yes, sir. Name is Keswick, Horace Keswick, of Johnson's artillery. We were overrun and captured in that engagement with Hancock. Here, turn around and let me get those ropes off your hands."

"Where are Johnson and Stewart now?" Mosby asked when his wrists were again free. "Are they here?"

"No, sir, the Yankees moved them out yesterday," Keswick replied, releasing Lovan. "I don't know where they took them.

Mosby thought for a moment. "Who's the ranking officer here in the stockade?"

"Guess that will be me, Major," Keswick answered.

"How many prisoners they got in here?" Lovan asked, still wondering about it.

"Four hundred and ten, last count. All the badly wounded are in another part of the camp."

Mosby wheeled slowly around, stared off toward the high, picket-like fence. Other men were stirring about in the darkness now, either awakened by the conversation in the doorway or unable to sleep for some reason.

"Captain," Mosby said, coming back to Keswick, "it is most important that Lovan and I get out of here. Not just because we don't want to be prisoners but because we are carrying an important message to General Breckinridge from General

Lee. It must be delivered. Have you explored all possibilities of escape?''

''We have,'' Keswick said. ''Only hope appears to be a tunnel. We're working on it now.''

Mosby's brows lifted. ''How soon . . .''

''Another twenty-four hours, if we're lucky.''

Mosby's voice reflected his disappointment. ''Be too late to help us.''

''That's for sure,'' Hob Lovan muttered. ''By noon tomorrow the major and me'll be stretchin' rope, if we ain't out of here.''

Keswick's head came up sharply. ''Why? Oh —I remember — that order Grant issued about all you Rangers. Major, I'm sorry, but I don't know what I can do to help. There's no chance at all of that tunnel being finished before tomorrow night — and maybe not then if the guards get to hanging around too close. They keep a tight watch . . .''

Mosby said, ''I know, Captain. They've doubled the sentries now, just for our benefit. Still doesn't change the problem, however. One guard or a hundred, we still must find a way out.''

They moved off into the darkness, walking slowly along the wall, stepping over the sleeping men as the Confederate leader studied the fence for possibilities. They made the entire circuit, could find no loophole. They halted again near the doorway to the barn. Mosby, feeling the hard pressure of fleeting time upon him, began to give the structure thorough consideration. He heard Keswick speak.

''Major, if you can come up with a plan, you'll find every man inside this stockade ready to help. Just say the word.''

"Appreciate that," the Ranger said. "Not going to be easy."

"You said something about a message from General Lee. Can you tell me what it's all about? Is there something big in the wind?"

Mosby considered the question. There was no reason he could see why the young officers should not know of the Confederate commander's intentions. Even if he were overheard by someone disloyal to the southern cause, or if there were a Yankee masquerading as a prisoner, it would be nothing new to the Union army staff. Thanks to Jasper Denning a full account of Lee's plans would be in their hands.

He recounted hurriedly the situation that faced the Army of Northern Virginia, pointing out the dire need for reinforcements and the absolute necessity for either Lovan or himself reaching Breckinridge with Lee's orders.

"And if you can pull off an escape here," he concluded, "get every soldier you can back to our lines. We need all we can muster."

"You can depend on it," Keswick said solemnly. "Important thing now though is to get you out of here."

Mosby was again studying the barn. "Was wondering about that roof. It's about ten feet from the edge, from the eaves, to the fence. If we had some rope and a man was to get up there, he might swing out and drop over the wall."

"Long jump," Keswick commented. "And it would be hard getting down the roof. It's plenty steep."

"That's where the rope would come in. Have to

throw it up from the opposite side and anchor it. Man could let himself down to the edge then."

Keswick shook his head. "Might scare up a little rope but wouldn't be near enough for that. All be short lengths of light stuff, like they tied around your wrists."

"Leaves one route open then," Mosby said. "It's the most risky but we'll have to chance it — over the fence."

"Just what I was thinkin'," Lovan said. "Get on top and jump down on the guards."

"Been tried before," Keswick said. "Men who did never got twenty yards before the sentries cut them down with their muskets."

"But this'll be different," the scout said, his voice grim. "They wasn't armed, likely, and we are. Them guards will never get the chance to throw lead at us."

"You've got weapons?" Keswick asked, surprised.

"The best kind," Lovan replied. He reached inside his shirt, drew forth a long sliver of steel whetted on both sides to a razor's edge. Unlike other Rangers who carried their knives in secret boot sheaths, he preferred to keep his under his left arm where it was held in place by a narrow band of cloth that encircled his chest. The blade had no handle, as did the usual knife, that end simply being unsharpened.

Keswick touched the point of the weapon gingerly. "Wicked," he murmured. "Knew you Rangers had a lot of tricks up your sleeve, never suspected anything like this, however." He glanced at Mosby. "You armed the same way, Major?"

For reply Mosby leaned down, drew his knife from its boot pocket. It was similar to that carried

by Lovan with the exception that the officer had re-
tained the handle.

Keswick smiled, shook his head. "You've got
the answers, all right. Only thing will be getting to
the top of the fence without being heard."

"No problem there," the Ranger chief said.
"But we'll need help. Two big men, tall ones. We'll
have to stand on their shoulders."

The captain thought for a moment. "Know just
the pair," he said.

"Fine. Get them."

Keswick disappeared into the barn. He was back
in a few minutes bringing with him two large,
powerfully built men, obviously of German descent.

"Couple of my artillerymen," he told the Rangers. "Herman and Ludwig Poppe. They handled
cannon for me."

They shook hands all around. Mosby outlined
what was to be done. Ludwig Poppe said, "Such
will be easy, Major."

"Next thing," Mosby continued. "is to pick out
the best place to make the attempt. Which side of
the stockade is nearest to the woods or cover of
some sort."

"The rear," Keswick replied promptly. "You'll
find a hundred yards of open ground, all down
slope. Then you're in brush and trees."

"Sure wish we had some horses waitin'." Lovan
said, morosely. "Walkin's gettin' mighty old."

"We'll find a couple," Mosby answered. "Important thing is to get over that wall. We ready?"

"Ready," Keswick said. "Follow me."

They circled the barn, came to the back wall of
the stockade. Mosby motioned for silence, then

moved up to the logs. He placed his ear against the rough surface, listened carefully. He could hear nothing and, after a few moments, dropped back to the others.

"Got to know just where the sentries are standing," he said. He touched Herman Poppe on the arm and together they went to the fence. The Ranger climbed onto the man's thick shoulders, peered cautiously over the top of the sharpened poles. The guards were as before; one at each corner, with the additional man now stationed in the exact center between. Pausing long enough to get a good diagram of the adjoining land in his mind, Mosby slipped from the German's shoulders.

Once again on the ground he said, "Hob, take the guard in the middle. I'll handle the one to our right. Man standing at the far end, the left, is slightly around to the side. With luck he won't hear us when we drop and will never know what's happening." The Ranger hesitated, laid a hand on the scout's arm. "This will be a close one. No need telling you to move fast — and don't miss."

"For a fact," Lovan said. "We sure don't want no musket blastin' off and awakin' the whole danged camp."

"Minute we're over," Mosby continued, facing Keswick, "you men get back inside the barn. Go hard with you if they find out you helped us."

"They won't know," the captain said. "And they can't punish us all. Or maybe they can but it won't matter." He reached for Mosby's hand and then that of Hob Lovan. "Good luck to you both. If this works and the other guards don't get wise, we'll follow. If they do, we'll still go out by the tunnel tomorrow night. One way or another we'll rejoin General Lee.''

Mosby said, ''Fine, Captain. And good luck to you.''

They slipped in closer to the fence, maintaining a strict silence. Mosby indicated the position of the Yankee sentry placed at the center of the wall to Lovan. With Keswick and the other Poppe brother, he made his way to the corner. He halted there, took his knife in hand and climbed onto the German's shoulders. Taking care not to lose balance, he motioned for Poppe to move in nearer. He reached for the pointed tips of the logs, steadied himself. The big artilleryman's height made it easy for him to gain the top.

Poised, he glanced toward Hob Lovan. The scout was a soft blur on the summit of the fence. He was awaiting the signal to strike. Mosby drew himself onto the ends of the logs. He looked down at the guard directly below. The man was leaning against the fence, his musket an arm's length away. Mosby lifted his hand, held it high to be sure Lovan would see it.

He brought it down suddenly — and launched himself at the Yankee sentry.

Chapter Seven

The scrape of Mosby's boots against the tips of the logs brought the guard around abruptly. The Ranger chief had a flashing glimpse of the man's startled, upturned face, and then he was upon him and they were going down in a tangle of flailing arms and legs.

Mosby rolled clear, bounded to his feet. The sentry, prone, slightly dazed, fumbled with his pistol. Mosby kicked out, sent the weapon skittering off into the darkness. The Yankee made a frantic stab for the knife in his belt. Mosby leaped forward. He swung his balled fist, putting every ounce of strength he had behind it. The guard groaned as the blow connected with his jaw. His head snapped back and he went sprawling full length.

A musket shot ripped through the night. Mosby spun in dismay. It had come from the direction of Hob Lovan. Relief swept through him when he saw the lithe, crouched figure of the scout spurt from the deep shadows along the wall and break for the trees beyond the cleared ground.

He followed immediately, cutting across the

field diagonally. They would have to move fast now. The sentry's shot would arouse the camp and they could expect instant pursuit. It was an unfortunate turn of luck that a warning had been sounded, but at least they were again free — and Hob wasn't wounded.

They gained the trees together. Back at the stockade voices were shouting, lanterns were bobbing through the darkness. Somewhere on the far side of the picket wall horses were getting under way, the hammering of their hooves sounding like drum beats.

"You all right, Major?" Lovan cried as they plunged headlong into the brush.

"All right — but you? That shot . . ."

"Danged musket went off when the sentry fell on it. Think maybe he shot hisself . . ."

They rushed on taking no care to move quietly, intent only on putting as much distance between themselves and the Yankee camp as possible before they were compelled to pause for breath.

"Which way?" Lovan gasped, beginning to falter. "To Germanna Ford?"

"No," Mosby answered. "First place they'll look. We'll have to cross the river somewhere else."

They heard the Yankees at that moment. They were pounding across the cleared ground, headed for the point where Mosby and the scout had entered the wood. Apparently other sentries, attracted by the gunshot, had seen the Confederates when they fled and noted the route they had taken.

Mosby swung hard right. They had been fleeing in a north-westerly direction. Now, to get out from under the oncoming Yankees, he turned east. That course would take them parallel to the Rapidan, rather than to its banks, but he could afford to take no chances. Later, once they had shaken the cavalrymen, they could swing back.

The racket of the approaching riders grew louder. Despite the dense brush and tree growth, the horses were breaking through at a fast gait. Mosby and Lovan, hunched low, called on their screaming muscles for more speed.

"Spread out! Spread out!"

It was Amos Neill's harsh voice. It echoed through the grove, sought out every hidden corner. How many men were with the sergeant Mosby could not tell. A half a dozen or so, judging from the noise.

"Keep bearin' toward the river! They'll be tryin' to make the ford!"

"Sergeant!"

It was Jasper Denning. The officer must have been somewhere nearby and immediately joined the chase.

"Slow your men down! You'll overrun them."

"Yes, sir, Lieutenant," Neill called back.

The non-com's voice seemed farther to the left and somewhat forward. Mosby's hopes rose. It appeared they might be slipping out from beneath the Yankees. He glanced at Lovan. The scout was trotting doggedly on, head low, mouth gaped as he fought for breath. Suddenly he tripped, went down. There was a loud crackle of brush. Instantly Mosby dropped beside him. Somewhere off to one side a man yelled.

"Who's that?"

Mosby hesitated. He had started to answer, to imitate a Yankee's nasal voice, then thought better of it. The soldier who had sung out could be the end rider in the line and be aware that no one in his party was beyond him. It was better to remain silent.

With Lovan breathing heavily beside him, the Ranger waited out the tense moments. All was quiet. The cavalryman had evidently halted when he heard the scout fall, was now listening into the darkness for more sounds.

"All right — all right, keep comin'!" Neill's voice was fainter. "Watch sharp! They're in here somewheres!"

Mosby heard the dry squeak of saddle leather, the faint jingle of bridle metal. Then came the slow, regular *tunk-a-tunk* of a horse walking across soft ground. The Ranger heaved a sigh. The man was at last moving on.

"Close," he murmured.

"Too danged close," Lovan agreed, shaking his head. "And all on account of me bein' so blamed slough-footed."

"Never mind," Mosby replied, listening for any more indications of Neill and his men. "The way we were running through that brush it's a wonder we both didn't end up with broken legs."

He could hear nothing. "They've swung to the ford," he said after a time. "Puts them away from us. We'll cut straight to the river. Ought to bring us out a half a mile or so below them."

They arose and pushed on. Shortly after midnight they reached the Rapidan, glowing dull silver in the pale starlight, and running high and broad with spring rains.

"Man'll be busy as a buzz saw in a pine knot,

crossin' that," Lovan said, cocking his head to one side. "She's movin' mighty fast."

"Don't see any other solution," Mosby answered. "Can you make it?"

"Well, never did take much to water but this won't be the first time I've had to paddle my way across a crick. You think Denning and his bunch will be watchin' the ford?"

"You can bet on it. They figure it's our only chance to . . ."

Mosby checked abruptly. The distinct sounds of an approaching horse had reached them through the darkness.

"Down!" the Ranger hissed and threw himself into the shadows beneath a clump of brush.

Lovan was with him instantly. Prone, they watched the trail along the river bank. A lone cavalryman appeared, riding slowly, his eyes searching back and forth.

"Be no trouble, knockin' him off that horse . . ."

Mosby said, "No, let him go. One horse wouldn't help us on this side of the river. And if he doesn't report back to the others when they expect him, it will give us away. Then we'd have Neill, Denning and the whole patrol down on us again. Let him be. When he returns and gets out of sight, we'll cross."

The Yankee moved by, continued along the edge of the river. Mosby and Lovan remained where they lay. A quarter hour dragged by . . . Again they heard the dull thud of a walking horse. They watched the cavalryman pass, waited out another ten minutes and then, crawling from the brush, made their way to the river.

Mosby waded in without hesitation. Soft splashes behind him told him that Lovan was not far away. The river deepened almost immediately and then they were soon over their depths. Quietly they began to swim, using long, underwater strokes and allowing the current to do most of the work.

They gained the opposite shore a long two hundred yards below their starting point but that was of no consequence to them. They had been able to cross without being seen by the Yankees and that was all that counted. Mosby, however, forever cautious and never taking anything for granted while in enemy territory, approached the river bank with care. When he felt solid ground beneath his feet, he motioned to Lovan and together they slipped into a dense overhang of vines, and halted.

"Denning could have sent some of his men to patrol this side," the Ranger chief whispered.

"Just what I was thinkin'," Lovan replied.

They waited, still partly submerged, and well hidden in the vines. Hearing nothing after a reasonable length of time, they pulled themselves onto the bank, the chilly water streaming from them in a dozen steady rivulets, and once more stopped. Again they listened into the dark. There was nothing save the usual and expected noises of the night.

They moved off into the wood, Mosby taking his directions from the stars and pointing now due west. They had been lucky — but they had lost valuable time.

"Clarksville is on ahead," he said as they hurried on through the brush. "We'll get horses there."

"Be mighty thankful for that," Lovan grunted.

"Been quite a spell since I done this much travelin' on my own legs."

They continued in silence after that. An hour later they came to the road, crossed over without incident, and once again plunged into a deep forest. The miles wore by. Their wet clothing dried on them, became stiff, then soft again as it chafed against their skin. Light began to streak the eastern sky, and the few birds still remaining in the war ravaged area, began to stir.

They came to a farmhouse, skirted it. There would be no help there. The Union army had marched straight through the country after the battle of the Wilderness and now it was under complete Yankee domination. Those farmers who elected to remain on their property despite the soldiers were under close surveillance and to ask help from any of them would be proposing a man take a dangerous risk.

Near the middle of the morning, as they were making their way along a badly overgrown hedgerow, Hob Lovan touched Mosby lightly on the arm.

"Major, there's somebody on our trail!"

The Ranger chief halted instantly. "You sure of that?"

"Middlin' sure."

Mosby pointed to a thick stand of ragged cedar, drew off into it. He had been so engrossed in his thoughts he had given little attention to anything else. "What makes you think so?"

"Heard a horse grunt, like they do when they jump a log or somethin'. Reckon it's Denning and that loudmouthed sergeant?"

Mosby nodded. "Just about have to be. They

could have picked up our trail where we crossed the road.''

''Maybe we ought to wait them out.''

Mosby considered the suggestion. ''We can't be far from Clarksville now,'' he said, finally. ''And I don't think they know for sure we're ahead of them. Let's keep going. Long as we've got brush between us and them, they won't spot us.''

They hurried on, traveling at a slow trot and careful to keep in the trees and bushes. They heard no more of the cavalrymen, if they were on their trail, and late in the morning they broke out into a small valley in which a cluster of houses lay. Mosby halted in the fringe of shrubbery.

''Clarksville,'' he said.

''And nothin' but open ground all the way to it,'' the scout grumbled. ''Why do people always have to chop down the trees when they build a town?''

''One thing to do,'' Mosby said. ''Run. We've got to get there before Denning, if he's behind us, sees us.''

''Could be Yankee soldiers down there.''

Mosby shook his head. ''Sure can't tell from here. Don't see any signs of them — horses and the like. Anyway, we'll have to chance it. We can't wait. Move straight for that barn ahead. It will keep us hidden from the street most of the way. You ready?''

''Ready as I'll ever be,'' Lovan replied. ''Let's go.''

Chapter Eight

They reached the rear of the barn, halted. It was a brief pause, however, for the likelihood of Jasper Denning and his cavalry being close on their heels stood foremost in John Mosby's mind. They circled the building and came around to the front. It was the last structure on the street and somewhat apart from the remainder of the town, a hundred yards or so farther along.

"Place sure does look deserted," Lovan commented as they studied the silent village.

"Yankees passed through here several days ago," Mosby said, frowning. "Things should have settled down to normal by now. Take a look inside the barn, see if there are any horses."

Lovan slipped off soundlessly toward the entrance to the building. Mosby turned his attention again to the town. It was strange. There should be someone around, someone on the street; children, women, old men. And if the Union army had left occupying troops, there would be signs of them.

Lovan moved back to his side. "Barn's plumb

empty. Ain't been no horses or nothin' else in there for a long spell. You see anybody yet?''

Mosby shook his head. "Not a soul."

"Don't seem to be nobody on our back trail, either. Had me a look through the window of the barn. All clear that direction."

"Let's find the town hall," Mosby said. "Ought to be somebody there."

"If there's anybody left," the scout added.

They started off, keeping to the rear of the buildings, deeming it unwise to show themselves on the street until they were absolutely certain of conditions. The houses were oddly quiet, deserted, yet they showed evidence of habitation — a housewife's washing hanging on a line — a pile of freshly split kindling — a door standing open . . .

They reached the center of the village. Mosby felt his uneasiness grow, but the need for horses was urgent. They could never hope to reach Breckinridge, somewhere beyond Massanutten Mountain in the Shenandoah Valley, in time unless they had mounts.

"There's the town hall," Lovan said, coming to a stop.

Mosby followed his leveled finger. It was a small, white building, standing on a corner. A weather-faded notice board bearing several tattered papers and dodgers was near the entrance.

"Somebody here," the scout murmured. "There's horses 'round back at the hitch rail."

At that moment the door to the building opened. A man sauntered out, casually glanced down the street and then settled down on a bench placed against the wall.

"Guess that's the answer," Mosby said. "There's a meeting going on. Everybody's inside."

"We goin' to join in?"

Mosby studied the man on the town hall porch. "Like to know just who's in there first. Don't want to walk in on a bunch of Yankee soldiers."

"Be a mite hard, havin' that look-see. Windows are all too high, and with that apple-knocker a settin' there . . ."

"Let's talk to him," Mosby said, realizing they could delay no longer. "He's not wearing a uniform. Expect he's one of the local residents — but keep your hand close to your pistol, just in case . . ."

Faint sounds back up the street in the vicinity of the barn brought the Rangers around. Three horsemen had pulled up before the deserted structure. Mosby recognized all in a quick glance; Denning, his partner, Oliver Moon, and the big Yankee sergeant, Amos Neill.

"They was follerin' us, sure as shootin'," Lovan said. "Major, we better do somethin' mighty quick."

Mosby swore softly. Another ten minutes and they would have been in the clear. They could have obtained horses and been on their way. He watched the lieutenant and his two companions wheel about and move slowly for the entrance to the barn. He spun to Lovan.

"Quick — cross the street! While they're looking the other way."

They ran swiftly, reached the corner of the town hall, drew themselves out of sight. The civilian on the bench watched them with indolent curiosity. Mosby glanced toward the barn. It was partly blocked by another building. As long as he and Lovan remained close to the front of the hall, they could not be seen by the Yankees. Nodding to the scout, the Ranger slipped around the corner and stepped up to the man on the bench.

"You live here in Clarksville?"

The civilian, a squat individual in dusty clothing and with an untidy, tobacco stained beard, shrugged. "Maybe."

"We're in the market for a couple of horses," Mosby said. "Who owns those out back?"

The man stirred himself. "Belong to some folks inside," he said, ducking his head at the closed door.

Mosby threw an anxious look in the direction of the barn. Denning, finding the structure empty, would be coming on into town shortly. There was no time to waste.

"Who's inside the building?" he asked, impatiently. "Any Yankees? Speak up, man — we're in a hurry!"

"Figured that," the bearded man grunted. "Nope, ain't no Yankees around here. You huntin' some?"

"Last thing we want to find," Mosby said, hanging on to his temper. "We're with the Confederate army. We need horses."

"Then I reckon you'd better go on inside," the civilian said, getting to his feet. "You can talk to the boys that owns them you saw. Don't know as they'll sell but you can find out . . ."

Mosby pressed the latch, pushed the door inward. Lovan moved up behind him. They entered a small foyer, faced a second closed door. Mosby opened it, looked into a larger chamber. Chairs lined the walls and formed rows across its center. There were two long tables at the front of the room upon which had been piled an assortment of items; clothing, silverware, household articles, some food.

The Ranger came to an abrupt stop, alarm bursting through him in a sudden flash. Two dozen or so persons, mostly women, children, a few old men, turned to face him. He heard Hob Lovan mutter something under his breath. And then two men, both roughly dressed and holding cocked pistols, rose from behind the tables.

"Come right in, gents," the taller of the pair drawled. "Name's Hunt. My boys and me've been watchin' you ever since you got to town. We're doin' a little collectin'."

Mosby remained frozen. His eyes moved to the townspeople gathered in the room, back to the accumulation of items on the tables, to the faces of Hunt and the man next to him. Understanding came swiftly. Hunt and his men were scavengers — outlaws of the worst sort. They moved in on helpless towns, looted them of what few valuables they still possessed. With all able-bodied men off at war, the renegades usually had an easy time of it.

"You don't hear me, gents?" Hunt called, wagging his revolver suggestively. "Step right up and make your deposit."

Mosby felt the hard, round muzzle of a pistol jab into his back, saw Hob Lovan flinch as the same treatment was accorded him. It was the man who had been on the porch.

"What they got to donate, Pete?" Hunt asked.

"You already look them over? Don't see no guns."

"Wasn't carryin' any. Said they was lookin' to buy a couple of horses. Reckon that means they got money."

"Money!" Hunt echoed, a pleased smile breaking across his unwashed face. "That's sure the best thing of all! Now, you gents hustle up here and unload. Dump everythin' you got on the table where I can see it."

Mosby's glance swept the frightened features of the townspeople. Anger flooded through him in a quick surge. He took a half step backward, felt Pete's weapon dig savagely into his spine.

"Careful, mister," the outlaw warned softly. "I'd as soon blow you loose from your backbone as draw my next breath."

"Three more comin', Hunt," a voice said from one of the windows. "Yankee soldiers."

The renegade leader circled the table in long strides. "Get out front, Pete," he said hurriedly. "Sure got to welcome our boys in blue — we want their guns and uniforms. I'll take care of these birds."

Chapter Nine

Hunt motioned imperiously at Mosby and Lovan. "Get over there with the rest — and no funny business, you hear? Try somethin' and we'll start shootin' right smack into the lot of you. Be plenty who'll get hurt."

The Rangers crossed the room, took places up against the wall. There was little else they could do at the moment but obey. Mosby glanced at an elderly gentleman with flowing white hair and a spade beard who stood next to him.

"How long has this been going on?"

The old man waited until Hunt had returned to his place behind the table where he crouched down out of sight, as before. He shook his head.

"They rode in last night and took over the town. This morning they routed everybody out and gave us orders to bring all we had that was worth anything here to the town hall. They've been a little worked up over it because there's not much of value left. Say they're going to look through all the houses and if they find anything that's been held back, they'll burn the town down. You know who they are?"

Mosby said, "No, except there's a lot more like them roaming the country. They follow the army, plunder and loot every chance they get."

"When I saw you — I thought you and your friend there were part of their gang . . ."

A woman sitting directly in front of Mosby, turned a fearful, strained face to him. "After they've got all they want — what will they do to us?"

"Nothing," Mosby replied, calming her anxiety. "They'll probably ride on. They won't harm you unless you give them cause."

"Thieving pigs!" the old man muttered. "If I were twenty years younger . . ."

Mosby felt the woman's eyes upon him, intent and searching. He heard her speak again.

"Aren't — aren't you Major Mosby — the Confederate Ranger?"

He hesitated momentarily, then nodded slightly. "Yes, I'm John Mosby. It will be better if you don't mention it," he added.

Relief spread across her features. She turned, leaned toward the woman in the next chair, whispered excitedly. Instantly his name rippled through the room. Mosby became aware of quick, covert glances flung at him, of the sudden stir, the brightened faces. The man with the spade beard put their hopes into words.

"Mosby, eh? Thank God you happened by! Now we'll show these brigands what's what!"

Mosby shifted uncomfortably. Without pistols or muskets there was nothing he and Hob Lovan could do to aid the people of Clarksville. Hunt and his renegades were all heavily armed and would not hesitate to use their weapons at the slightest provocation.

And too, there was the ever pressing need to keep moving, to get Lee's message to General Breckinridge. He could not afford to get involved in any incident that would consume any considerable amount of time. If a means for escape from Hunt — and now from Jasper Denning and his men — presented itself, he must seize it. His first obligation was to Lee and the Confederate army.

Outside, in the street, he could hear the low mutter of voices. It would be Denning, with Sergeant Neill and Oliver Moon, talking with the outlaw, Pete. They would be entering shortly and the matter would become further complicated.

The old man with the spade beard said, "Always wished I'd been young enough to join up with you, Mosby. You're doing my kind of fighting — you Rangers. Lot of satisfaction riding around the country, helping out people in trouble and stinging the Yanks every chance you get. It's a great way to be living!"

John Mosby winced. Too many assumed the life of a Ranger was all romance and adventure. Too many thought there was little else to it than racing through the forests and across the valleys like knights of old, seeking out the distressed, the helpless to aid while all the time they were making sport of the enemy.

They overlooked the hardships, the privation, the days and nights without food; the unavailability of medical care if wounded, the endless training in silent warfare and, above all, the ever-present shadow of death. They had no conception of what it was like to have thousands upon thousands of men on the alert for you, hopeful of a chance for ambush or any other means to kill you.

The Rangers had become so deep a thorn in the side of the Union army that special efforts had been undertaken to apprehend and annihilate Mosby and his men. Picked details of hard-riding cavalry had been assigned to the areas known to be frequented by the Rangers and generous rewards were being offered for information that would lead to their capture.

But to no avail. Mosby and his ghostlike riders had continued to harass the Federal forces, moving swift and often, seldom in the same place twice but always lurking somewhere in the shadowy background, ready to strike suddenly and effectively — and be gone.

And now that reputation for invincibility was catching up with him. Mosby could see it in the childlike faith and hope that shone in the eyes of the people of Clarksville. He would find a way to overcome Hunt and his band of scavengers; he would rescue them from the clutches of the outlaws and save their possessions. Of that they were convinced.

". . . There's a Clarksville boy in your battalion. Name of Jeremy Meyers. He . . ."

The outer door rattled. Denning and the others were coming. Hunt rose from behind the table, swept the room with his hard, bitter eyes.

"All of you — shut up that whisperin'! And don't be forgettin', anybody makes a false move . . ."

The inner door opened. The outlaw sank out of sight. Mosby watched Jasper Denning, closely followed by Neill and Oliver Moon, walk into the room and halt. Pete and another of the scavengers silently eased in behind them.

Sergeant Neill, Mosby saw, had appropriated his belt with its brass-studded holsters and two revolvers that had been taken from him back at Germanna Ford. He wore them low on his hips, the belt being too short to encircle his waist.

Denning glanced about the room, a questioning frown on his face. He caught sight of Mosby and Hob Lovan. His expression changed immediately.

"Well, Major — you didn't get far . . ."

At that moment Hunt rose into view. Pete and the man with him crowded up close to the Yankees, their pistols out. Hunt smiled amiably.

"Soldier boys, eh? Mighty happy to see you."

Lieutenant Denning's jaw hardened. "What's the meaning of this? Who are you? We're here on official business of the United States army . . ."

"Sure, sure, soldier boy — only I'm the one doin' the business. You just stand right where you are, unless you're tired of livin'. Pete, collect their pistols and trot them up here."

The outlaw moved to obey. He pulled the revolvers from the Yankees' holsters, carried them to the table. Hunt focused his attention on Neill.

"Get that there holster outfit too, Pete. Mighty fine lookin' leather workin'."

Mosby watched Neill unbuckle the belt and hand it to the renegade. It had been a gift from a Union soldier, a young private left for dead on the battle-field by his comrades. Mosby had found the boy and taken him to the home of some Confederate sympathizers where his wounds were treated. During convalescence the soldier had made the holsters and belt, taking great pains to engrave and decorate them. Later he had presented them to the Ranger as a token of his gratitude.

"Now you soldier boys just step up close and empty your pockets here on the table," Hunt said, when he had the belt set. "We're real interested in money, gents. I'll take all you got."

The outlaw leader swiveled his attention to Mosby and the scout as though suddenly recalling their presence. "You fellers get up here, too. This here little interruption sort of put you off for a minute, but I don't want you to feel slighted. All of you — step lively!"

Mosby and Lovan moved away from the wall, fell in beside the glowering Yankees and advanced to the tables.

"Shell out, gents!" Hunt said cheerfully, waving his pistol. "I'm expectin' everythin' you got on you. Even them uniforms you're wearin'," he added, halting his gaze on the soldiers.

He paused, laughed as Denning looked at him frowningly. "Now, don't you get upset, Lieutenant. My boys'll take you in the back room. Sure wouldn't want you shamin' none of the ladies here by undressin' in front of them. No, sir!"

Grimly silent the five men began to place their possessions on the table. Mosby had only a small amount of money on him, nothing else. Lovan could contribute little, also. Denning and Oliver Moon were the heavy losers, having with them gold watches, rings and considerable in Union green-backs. Neill had only a few things of value.

When they were finished Hunt pawed through the pile gleefully. "Now, that's what I call a right good haul! Got more here than the whole blamed town could dig up! All right, Pete, take these jaspers into the back room and get their clothes. We got to be pullin' out of this burg pretty soon."

Pete, with the assistance of the second outlaw, prodded Mosby and the others toward a door behind the renegade leader. He opened it and they entered, finding themselves in a small ante-chamber. Likely it was used for private meetings, Mosby guessed. There was no outside entrance, only a single, small window in one wall.

Pete faced them. "Start strippin' off your duds. I'll scare you up somethin' to put on."

"I'm not wearing any uniform," Mosby said. "Neither is my partner. That mean us, too?"

"Don't make no difference. We want what you got, anyway. Them boots you're sportin' look mighty good. And that shirt, too."

Lovan growled something. Pete wheeled to him. "What's eatin' you, grandpa? You don't like what's goin' on around here?"

"I sure as blazes don't!" the scout declared hotly. "If I had a chance . . ." His words died as he caught Mosby's eye.

Pete spat, touched them each with his glance. "Get busy," he said. "Old Hunt gets riled when people don't do what he tells 'em to. And we're in a hurry." He turned, re-entered the large room, pulling the door closed as he went.

"I'm damned if I'm handin' my uniform over to them scavengers!" Neill exploded. "They can do what they want, but I ain't takin' . . ."

John Mosby only half heard the sergeant's angry words. He moved quickly to the window, looked out into the yard. He had no idea of what could be done and the situation appeared hopeless; but he was a man accustomed to facing the impossible. He gave the window brief note. It was too small for any one of them to use as a means for escape. There were more outlaws outside, anyway.

"There's six horses at that rack," he said, coming back to the center of the room. "Three men are with Hunt. Leaves two more somewhere around the building." The Ranger paused, looked at the Yankees. "Any of you notice where they were stationed?"

Denning cast a disdainful look at Mosby. "We'll handle this. I don't care to get involved with you . . "

"Don't be a complete fool!" Mosby snapped impatiently. "We're in this together, whether you like it or not. And if we want to get out of it, we'll have to do it together — five of us against their six."

Moon said, "He's right, Jasper. Maybe if we all . . ."

"I'll consider it on one condition," the Yankee officer said stiffly, his eyes on Mosby. "You and your scout turn yourselves over to me as my prisoners and give me your word . . ."

"Forget it!" Mosby snapped. "We're not your prisoners and we wouldn't give you our parole if we were!"

"Then, by the saints, I'll make you a prisoner!" Neill yelled and lunged at Mosby.

The Ranger sidestepped quickly. As the sergeant reeled by he chopped him sharply on the back of the neck with the heel of his hand. Neill stumbled, went to his knees. He was up instantly, pure hatred flaming in his eyes.

"Wasn't for you — damn you — we'd not be in this mess!"

"Sergeant!" Denning barked. "Forget it! There's no time now . . ."

The door jerked open. Hunt, wearing Mosby's belt and pistols, entered. He carried his own weapon in his hand. His glance slid over the five men, halted on Lovan and the Ranger chief.

"Which one of you birds is Mosby?"

The Confederate officer nodded. "I am."

Hunt's thick lips cracked into a grin. "Well, now, that's what I call a piece of real good luck!"

"He's my prisoner," Denning broke in. "I'm taking him back to Union headquarters. You interfere and you'll be in serious trouble with the army of the United . . ."

"You won't be goin' nowheres, Lieutenant," Hunt said in a deadly calm voice, "unless I say so. Get that in your head. And you better get to peelin' off them uniforms. I ain't tellin' you again."

He came back to Mosby. "Come along with me, Mister Guerrilla Mosby. There's a fat reward for you over at that Yankee camp I'm aimin' to collect!"

Chapter Ten

Denning stared at the outlaw. "You try that and they'll throw you in the stockade so fast . . ."

"Now, why would they do that, Lieutenant?" Hunt drawled. "Ain't I just a loyal Yank a-doin' my bounden duty? I expect they'll be real glad to see me when they find out who I'm bringin' them."

The officer shook his head. "Somebody will recognize you. Better leave Mosby to me."

"Ain't nobody goin' to recognize me. Never been down this way before," Hunt said. "Come on, Reb, let's get movin'. You, too, old man," he added, glancing at Lovan. "Maybe they'll pay a reward for you, same as for him."

The outlaw opened the door, motioned toward it with his pistol. He looked at Denning. "Better start pullin' off them duds unless you want me to send in a couple of my boys to help!"

Mosby, with Hob Lovan at his shoulder, walked into the main part of the town hall. Everything was as he had last seen it; the people of Clarksville were still lined up against the wall or occupying a few of the chairs. Pete and two more of the renegades were mounting a close watch over them. If the six horses tethered to the rack behind the building were an accurate indication of the size of Hunt's gang, and there was no reason to believe they were not, there were still two men to be accounted for.

Mosby considered the advisability of making a try for escape at that moment. At least, outside the small cell-like anteroom the possibilities were better. Lovan and he still had their knives and the cocksure Hunt had grown slightly careless from his success. They might turn upon the outlaw leader, capture him. But to do so would endanger the townspeople. Pete and his friends would still hold the upper hand. To Hob's questioning eyes he shook his head slightly. They had no choice but to wait.

"I'm sorry, Major — I never meant . . ."

It was the old man with the spade beard. Apparently he had been the one who gave away Mosby's identity to the outlaws.

"It's all right," he said. "Forget it."

He felt Hunt's hand drop onto his shoulder, shove him roughly toward the center of the room. Anger flared through the Ranger, but he held tight to his temper. His time would come. He must be patient.

"Me and Pete are takin' this pair to the Yankees and claimin' the reward," Hunt said, placing his attention on the remaining two renegades. "You just set quiet here. Don't let nobody out — and keep an eye on them soldiers in the back room."

One of the outlaws said, "All right, but you better send in Ed and Joe. We'll be needin' their help."

Hunt swore scornfully. "What for? To keep watch over a bunch of old folks and kids? Naw — they best stay outside, just in case somebody else shows up."

"But them soldiers . . ."

"They ain't got no weapons, have they? What you feared of? They won't be tryin' anythin'. Come on, Pete, let's get started."

Mosby and Lovan, shepherded by the two scavengers, moved for the door. As they stepped out onto the porch fronting the building, Pete halted.

"They didn't have no horses. Just come walkin' in. You want they should use a couple of these?" he asked, pointing to the mounts Denning and the other Yankees had ridden.

"Sure not!" Hunt exclaimed. "You want to get us nabbed? Somebody might recognize them army horses, remember who they belonged to. We'll take a couple of our own." He paused, looked around. "Where's Ed?"

"Right here," a voice said from the corner of the building. "What's up?"

"Got us a couple of valuable prisoners," Hunt explained. "Pete and me are takin' them over and collectin' the reward the Yankee army's offerin'."

"What about the others?"

"The soldiers? They ain't worth nothin'. They're inside sheddin' their uniforms. You and Joe stay outside here, now, and keep watch. Charlie and Zeke can take care of the inside."

Ed grunted. "How long you figure to be gone?"

"Hard tellin'. Most likely be back some time after dark. There some rope around here handy?"

"In my saddlebags," Ed replied.

They circled the building, came to a halt beside the horses tethered to the rack. The sixth outlaw, the last, arose from the brush off to their left and ambled toward them. Hunt began his explanations and instructions once more.

Hob Lovan eased a half step nearer Mosby. "We better be doin' somethin', Major," he murmured. "Once they get us tied to them saddles . . ."

"Watch me," the Ranger replied in a whisper. "When I jump Hunt, you go for Pete."

Relief and satisfaction spread over the scout's seamy face. "Was a-startin' to worry a mite about it . . ."

Pete was rummaging through the leather pouches on one of the horses. Finally he produced a short coil of small size rope.

"Ain't much here," he said aloud, more to himself than Hunt. "About enough to tie their hands."

Mosby, tense and waiting, barely heard. He watched the outlaw leader closely. He must choose the exact moment, the time when all least expected anything. He saw Joe turn away, head back into the brush. Hunt started to wheel — and at that precise instant the Ranger lunged.

He struck Hunt with the full force of his spring. The outlaw yelled, went over backwards with Mosby on top. They hit the ground in a solid, jarring jolt. Mosby's right hand clawed at the revolver — his revolver — on the renegade's hip, jerked it free.

He rolled away, hearing the scuffle that was going on between Hob Lovan and Pete. There was no time to look, to see if the scout fared well or was in difficulty. He must act quickly — bearing in mind there was Joe to be reckoned with — as well as the man out front, Ed.

He saw Hunt draw himself up, bring his arm around for a hasty shot. Mosby fired point-blank. The outlaw's body leaped from the bullet's impact, slammed back to the ground. Another gunshot blasted through the warm, morning air. Dust spurted into Mosby's face. Joe!

The Ranger rolled in, keeping Hunt's lifeless shape between himself and the outlaw. Joe, still crouched in the brush, fired again. The ball dug into the turf only inches from the Ranger's head. He had a glimpse of Lovan rising to his feet, knife in hand. Pete lay motionless beyond him.

"His gun — get his gun!" Mosby shouted. The others, attracted by the shots, would be there soon. They would need every weapon.

Close beside Hunt, he drew his feet up under him, prepared to make a dash for the side of the building. He could not see Joe, hidden somewhere in the brush; he could only guess at his exact position. He raised up suddenly, threw two quick bullets toward the outlaw, and sprinted for the protection of the wall. He heard Lovan shoot, realized the scout was covering his retreat also, as he ran. Together they gained the shelter of the building.

"Get after the one up front," he gasped to Lovan. "I'll take care of Joe."

Lovan slipped off quickly toward the porch where the man called Ed was stationed. Mosby, dropping to his hands and knees, peered cautiously around the corner. He had to make his bullets count. He had no more on him; the rest were in his belt still around Hunt's body.

He saw movement at the far corner of the building. A man broke into the open, ran hard for the brush thicket in which Joe lay concealed. It was Ed.

Mosby took careful aim, pressed off his shot. The outlaw hesitated in stride, crumpled and fell. A shout went up from Joe. He leaped to his feet, oaths pouring from his lips as he began to empty his revolver at the Ranger. He staggered, swayed uncertainly, then disappeared from view.

Lovan! Mosby realized then that the scout had circled the building in search of Ed. When he failed to flush out the outlaw, he had gone on and had been close by when Joe exposed himself.

Mosby, thinking now of the two renegades inside the town hall, hurried to where Hunt lay. He rolled the man over, unbuckled his belt and holsters and drew them on. Lovan trotted up, a pistol in each hand.

"What about them other two?"

Mosby glanced at the back wall of the structure. Denning, Neill and Moon had crowded up to the window and were watching.

"Got to get them out of there somehow," he replied. "Can't leave those people trapped the way they are."

Lovan shook his head. "You forgettin' them Yankees? We'll be turnin' them loose to dog our tracks again."

"Know that," Mosby replied. "Can't be helped."

He wheeled to the horses, nervous from the

smoke and gunfire. He glanced over them quickly, selected two for their own use — a black for Lovan, a thick-bodied bay for himself. The remaining four he released, sent them galloping off into the brush with sharp slaps on the rump.

"When we get up front we do the same for Denning's horses," he said to Lovan. "May have to help them get free, but we sure don't have to make it easy for the Yankees to follow us."

The scout nodded his understanding. "One thing's a-botherin' me. How we goin' to get them polecats out of there without somebody gettin' hurt?"

Mosby shook his head. "All I know is that we've got to do it. The how of it comes next."

They started along the side of the structure for the front. Mosby was considering all possibilities but at every turn he came up against a black wall. There was only the one entrance; the windows were all too high and small to be of use. There was no upper floor or attic that might be reached from the roof. And to simply burst in, shoot it out with the renegades would be dangerous; some of the townspeople were certain to be struck by stray bullets.

At the corner of the building the Ranger halted abruptly as an idea flashed into his mind. If Denning had a weapon he could come from the anteroom, on signal, at the identical moment Lovan and he entered the front door. The outlaws, caught in between, would most likely surrender without a fight.

The drawback was apparent. It involved arming the Yankee officer — and that meant trouble for Lovan and himself. Once inside the main room of the town hall, Neill and Oliver Moon could seize weapons from the pile on the table. There was no doubt in Mosby's mind what would then follow; the soldiers would attempt to recapture their prisoners. He outlined the plan to the scout.

"Be puttin' our necks in a noose again," Lovan said promptly, recognizing the danger. "But if you want to chance it, I'm willin'. Say," he exclaimed, "just had me an idea. Why don't we just toss a couple of these extra pistols we got through the window to Denning? Let him handle it."

It was a good thought, one that very well could be the answer. Most likely, after he and Lovan had ridden off, the outlaws would flee, anyway.

"We can be on our horses, ready to line out of here," Lovan added. "Time they got outside, we'd be gone."

"Just what we'll do," Mosby said.

They wheeled about, started back along the wall of the building. They covered a half a dozen steps. Mosby heard Lovan say something, half turned to ask him to repeat it. The sudden, spiteful crack of gunfire shattered the quiet. There was a dull thud in the wooden planking near the Ranger's head. He whirled, instinctively dropped to a crouch. A second burst of gunshots rapped across the echoes of the first. Hob Lovan grunted in pain and fell to the ground.

Chapter Eleven

Mosby scoured the street, the brush beyond it, for a glimpse of the marksman — or marksmen. He was not sure how many there were, but he had a feeling it was the two outlaws he had assumed were still inside the town hall; they had played it smart and got out before they could become trapped.

"How bad are you hurt?" he asked, without looking at Lovan.

"Could've been worse," the scout replied. "Hit me in the leg — the danged bushwhackers! You spot 'em?"

"Not yet," Mosby said.

"Wonder if it ain't them other scavengers . . ."

Mosby made no answer. His gaze was fastened to the deep shadows in a passageway between two buildings on the far corner. He had seen motion — or thought he had. Flat on the ground he wormed his way about until he faced the structures. Lovan followed his eyes.

"You see somethin'?"

"Yes — across the street. Next to that . . ."

"There they go!" Lovan cried and fired almost as he spoke.

Mosby saw the two men at the same instant. They had leaped to their feet, begun to run, headed for a thick wedge of brush thirty feet or so farther down. Apparently they hoped to circle the town hall and reach their waiting horses by that route.

The Ranger chief's shot came a brief moment after that of the scout. The man ahead stumbled, plowed face forward into the dust. Hob Lovan fired again. The second renegade halted abruptly, spun half about, and then fell heavily.

Mosby did not hesitate. He got to his feet, leaned over to help Lovan. "Got to get out of here — Denning and his bunch will be coming!"

Lovan struggled to stand. The outlaw's bullet had struck him in the fleshy part of the leg. The wound was bleeding freely and needed attention but it was not too serious. He took a short step, went to one knee as the injured member gave way.

"Blast it!" he muttered. "Major, you better go on. I ain't goin' to be much account, nohow."

"Forget it!" Mosby snapped. "Throw your arm over my shoulder. Once you get on your horse you'll be all right."

"First got to get there," Lovan grumbled.

They hurried along the wall, the scout leaning against Mosby and limping badly. Inside the building all was quiet. Evidently Denning and his men were still in the back room and the townspeople, fearful of what the gunfire had meant, had not stirred.

The Rangers reached the end of the structure

and halted. The horses were at the rack. Mosby threw a glance toward the window. From their off-angle position he could not see if the Yankee lieutenant and his men were watching or not.

They must move quickly. The instant Denning and his men saw them mount their horses, they would realize the outlaws no longer were in control of the building. They would rush into the main room, seize their weapons and attempt to halt the escape. It would be close, Mosby knew. Hob Lovan was in no condition to act with any great amount of speed.

He wished now he had taken time to scatter the Yankees' horses. It had been his intention to do so. but the unexpected appearance of the outlaws had brushed it from his mind. Now it was too late.

He glanced at Hob Lovan. "Got to hit the saddle fast and pull out in a hurry. Denning will be watching."

"Expect I'll make it," the scout replied. "Point is, if I don't — you keep goin', Major. You got to get to Breckinridge."

Mosby said, "We'll make it together. Ready?"

"Whenever you are."

The Ranger delayed no longer. He took a firm grip about the scout's slim body with his arm and said, "Now."

They broke from the corner of the town hall, hurried across the open ground. At best it was slow going. Lovan's leg pained him intensely but he uttered no cry, simply clung to Mosby and hobbled on.

They reached the horses. Mosby boosted the scout onto the black, jerked the reins free and handed them up to Lovan. He ducked under the nervous animal's head and rushed to where the bay stood, flinging a glance at the window as he vaulted to the saddle. No one was visible. A momentary hope surged through him. They were in luck. The Yankees were not watching; they had chosen a moment when all were engaged elsewhere.

And then that feeling of optimism died. He heard a yell. Denning, closely followed by Moon and the sergeant, burst from the far corner of the building. A pistol cracked viciously. Mosby heard the drone of the bullet as it passed nearby.

He whirled his horse about. Lovan was already pulling away. The scout had twisted around, was leveling his revolver at the oncoming Yankees. Mosby heard the blast, saw one of the men — Moon he thought it was — go down. In the next fragment of time he was plunging into the brush with Lovan.

They drove on recklessly, gained a thick stand of trees, cut sharply to their right. Mosby glanced over his shoulder. Denning and the others were not in sight. Even the wounded man had been pulled back to safety on the far side of the town hall.

"We — made it . . ." Lovan said, grinning, striving to hide the pain that was shooting through his body at every lunge of his horse.

Mosby nodded, wheeled in close to the scout. He reached out, grasped Lovan's reins, pulled the black to a halt. The scout stared at him in amazement.

"Ain't no time to be stoppin'!"

"Take them a couple of minutes to get mounted," Mosby said, dropping from the saddle and drawing his handkerchief. In quick, deft motions he ripped it into strips, fashioned a bandage and wrapped it tightly about the scout's wound.

It was accomplished in moments and then he was again on the bay. "That'll hold you until we get to a farmhouse, or some place where we can get you doctored properly."

He spurred off through the grove with Lovan coming hard in his wake. He was heading directly west; they should be bearing more to the north, he knew, but for the time he deemed it best to take advantage of the thick cover.

A half hour later they pulled their winded horses to a walk. They were still in trees but now cleared fields were beginning to appear and the Ranger realized they would soon be faced with crossing open ground unless they wished to sacrifice time by swinging wide.

"You think we shook off them Yanks?" Lovan wondered as they pressed on steadily.

Mosby shrugged. "Good chance of it. We had a fair start — and you slowed them down by winging one of them. Big problem is that Denning knows where we're headed. He can figure just about where we'll be."

The scout nodded. "Another good reason why you ought to go on alone, leave me to head 'em off."

"Wouldn't help," the Ranger chief said, again dismissing the suggestion. Regardless of what Hob Lovan said, he was not abandoning him.

They came to the end of the grove and halted. Before them stretched a broad valley, devoid of brush and other cover. It extended for miles in all directions.

"Take too long to circle," Mosby said, thinking aloud. "And if Denning is on our trail, he's bound to see us before we can get to the other side." He turned, glanced at Lovan. "How's the leg?"

The scout said, "Fine. Quit bleedin'. Don't worry none about me."

"Got to cross this valley fast. Think you can manage a gallop until we've reached the trees on the yonder side?"

"I'll make it," Lovan said grimly.

Mosby grinned at the old scout. "All right, take off. I'll be right behind you."

Lovan threw Mosby a sharp look, instantly comprehending the Ranger's thinking. He started to protest but Mosby wheeled around to his rear, slapped the black hard on the rump. The animal bolted into the open.

Mosby followed. The two horses, rested somewhat after their earlier efforts, ran easily over the smooth, sloping ground. They dropped down the near grade, gained the floor of the valley, began the gentle climb up the opposite side. Lovan was leaning forward on his saddle, favoring his wound by resting his weight on his good leg and one hand locked about the pommel. His leathery face was taut but he never slackened his pace.

Half way up the slope Mosby, prompted by some inner warning mechanism, turned about and looked to their back trail. He saw two horsemen break into view, halt momentarily in the fringe of brush, and then start down into the valley. Two men — in Yankee blue uniforms. There was no mistaking their identity.

Denning and the big sergeant, Amos Neill.

Chapter Twelve

Tension gripped John Mosby. He looked ahead. The trees were a long hundred yards away. That Denning and Neill had not seen them was inconceivable but, thanks to the lead they had on the Yankees, they should reach the grove safely.

They should — barring an accident.

He glanced at the old scout. He was hanging grimly to the saddle of his galloping horse. Every motion of the animal was driving pain through his body, Mosby knew; that he could not go much longer without some medical attention being given the wound was also evident.

They thundered up the slope, came to the first outcropping of brush. The horses began to slow as they left the smooth floor of the valley and entered the dense tangle of brush and trees. Lovan twisted about, turned his gaunt face to Mosby. He started to speak, saw the two Yankees in the distance beyond the Ranger chief. His jaw clamped shut, he shook his head and resumed the task of staying aboard the black.

Mosby spurred up beside him. "Hang on!" he

shouted. "We'll give them the slip and then get that leg of yours fixed up!"

Lovan nodded woodenly. "Better you keep goin'," he replied. "Leave them Yankees to me."

"No need for that," Mosby said and pulled away.

They rode into the forest in a direct, straight line. A quarter mile inside, with the horses again showing signs of wear, and a thick screen of shrubbery between them and the valley, Mosby swung right.

They pushed their mounts at a steady trot for a time, then allowed them to drop to a quiet walk. It was better to move softly now and forget speed, since they were no longer in front of Denning and Neill. Mosby's one hope was to pull off to the side and permit the Yankees to override them.

"There they go!"

Jasper Denning's voice was a sudden stab of unexpected sound in the afternoon quiet. Mosby whirled, threw a glance to the side. The officer was so near he could see the glitter of his uniform buttons. Sheer chance had brought the Yankees into the grove at a lower point; and by pure luck they had intercepted the course Mosby and Hob Lovan had taken.

A gunshot smashed through the trees. The ball clipped foliage close by the Rangers. Mosby dug his heels into the bay's flanks, sent the husky little horse plunging off after Lovan, already rushing deeper into the brush.

Denning yelled again. There was no reply from Neill and this set up a worry within Mosby. He had seen no sign of the sergeant, did not know his exact position. He could be above or below the Yankee lieutenant.

"Left!" Mosby shouted at Lovan. "Cut left!"

He saw the scout, weaving unsteadily on the racing black, obediently swing off. A rider burst into view to their right. Neill! He had guessed correctly. Had they not altered course they would have ridden straight into the sergeant.

Neill jerked his horse to a skidding halt, pulling the animal to its haunches. He snatched at his pistol, brought it up for a quick shot. Mosby, throwing himself to one side, snapped a bullet at the Yankee, taking no time to aim.

The ball struck the earth just ahead of the sergeant's horse, sent up a shower of dust and litter. The animal shied violently, nearly unseating the cavalryman as it went dancing sideways into the shrubbery.

"Watch them! Watch them!"

Jasper Denning's voice echoed through the grove on the tail of Mosby's gunshot. He was somewhere to the left now, coming up fast. The hammering of his horse's hooves, the crackling of the brush, made his position easy to pinpoint.

Mosby, with Lovan a dozen yards ahead of him, fled farther into the wood. Their one chance was to get as deep in the dense growth as possible, and again try to swerve off and let the Yankees bypass them. But it had not worked the first time — it could fail again.

"This way!"

It was Neill's harsh, booming voice summoning Denning. Mosby looked anxiously at Hob Lovan. How the scout was managing to stay on the saddle was difficult to understand. Plunging headlong through the tangled forest was hard even for a man in full possession of his strength and faculties; for one weakened by loss of blood and wracked by pain it was nothing short of miraculous.

But Lovan, despite his sheer determination, could not keep it up much longer. He must be allowed to halt, to rest and get medical attention. Mosby urged his horse forward until he was alongside the scout's black. He peered closely at Lovan's strained features. Hob seemed barely conscious. He was acting from instinct, hanging on simply by willpower. The knuckles of his right hand, which clutched the pommel of his saddle, showed white from the intensity of his locked grasp.

Mosby listened for Neill and Denning. He could hear them crashing through the brush not too far behind. He could not see either of the two. He moved in closer to Lovan again.

"Turn off when we reach that stand of oak," he cried, pointing to a low, thick band of scrubby trees a short distance ahead. "Hide out — I'll lead them off and cut back later."

Lovan nodded, his face drawn with pain.

"Won't take me long. I'll whistle when it's all clear."

The Ranger chief slowed, dropped back a few yards. He allowed Lovan to pull ahead but kept himself in full view. The success of the plan depended upon the Yankees seeing him and following. He watched the scout draw abreast of the oak thicket and curve into it. He then altered his own path, angled off into an opposite direction.

"There they go!"

He heard Neill sing out, had a momentary fear

that Lovan might have been seen as he turned off. He spurred the bay to a gallop and rode deeper into the grove. Neill and Denning both opened up with their pistols but Mosby's erratic flight and the dense shrubbery combined to make their efforts useless.

The Ranger, bending low and pressing his mount for its best, rushed on through the forest, now beginning to darken with afternoon shadows. He thundered across a narrow clearing, splashed through a shallow stream. A low swell lay before him. He pounded to the crest, feeling the bay begin to weaken and wilt under him.

He glanced back. Neill and Denning were still coming on. Relief swept through him. They had not seen Hob Lovan cut off; they had swallowed the bait.

He clattered down the rock-strewn slope of the hillock, favoring the bay now as much as possible as he swerved to the left. Without Lovan to consider it was easier to maneuver, to lace back and forth through the brush in an effort to confuse the Yankees.

He saw open ground ahead. It did not look to be as large as the valley had been. More likely it was a field, once part of some farm and probably a hundred yards or so across. A tight grin crossed his face. If he could make it to the far side without a Yankee bullet catching up with him, it would be easy to shake Neill and Denning. After that he would simply double back over the field at its far edge unnoticed.

It was the crossing that lay ahead now that would be risky. Out in the open he would present an easy target for the two men, unless he was beyond pistol range — and that he did not know. But he had no choice, regardless.

He leaned forward over the bay, called upon the weary horse for a final burst of speed. The bay responded. They bolted into the clearing, started over the smooth, grassy ground at a hard gallop. Halfway Mosby heard the Yankees. He looked back, saw them emerge from the brush. They began to shoot immediately. Bullets droned nearby. He crouched lower. The bay seemed to realize the danger, somehow lengthened his stride.

He should be conserving some of the horse's strength he knew, for once they gained the far side of the field — *if* they gained it — he would still be faced with the problem of eluding his pursuers. But he was not too worried about that. The brush appeared dense and the day was growing old. The deep shadows in the grove would be his ally.

The heavier, booming sound of a musket and the loud whirr of a ball jarred Mosby's thoughts. He threw a quick glance over his shoulder. Neill had a rifle and was now using it. The Ranger had not considered that possibility — but of course the cavalry sergeant would be carrying one on his saddle. Evidently he had been waiting for just such an opportunity to make use of it. He saw Neill reload hastily, doing it expertly as he steadied himself on his horse with his knees. There was a dull flash of sunlight on the weapon's barrel as the Yankee swung it up for a second try.

Mosby veered sharp left, heard an angry buzz as the musket ball passed by him, smashed into a clump of bushes only a few paces ahead. He raised his eyes. The grove was still a dozen yards away. Neill could possibly reload and get off a third shot — and this time, if he decided to target the bay instead of the man . . .

The Ranger swung hard left, broke stride. He jerked the bay back to the left, swerved again to the right. It was costing precious time and distance but Neill would have no easy shot. He heard the musket crack once more, held his breath for a fragment of time. There was no sound of a whirring bullet and he knew he was safe. Neill had missed cleanly. And the trees were just a step away.

In full view of the Yankees John Mosby curved into the grove. He went straight on for twenty yards, cut back at right angles. He covered another fifty yards, came into a small ravine. Thick with berry bushes, it offered the cover he sought. He pulled to a halt.

Dismounting, he drew both revolvers and waited. He heard the Yankees enter the grove, slow their horses to a walk. Neill shouted something but he could not make it out. Denning's reply, coming from farther left, was equally unintelligible. After that there was silence broken only by the deep sucking and wheezing of the bay as he struggled to recover his spent wind.

Mosby let a full quarter hour elapse. There had been no further sounds from the Yankees and he guessed it was safe to assume they had moved on, were searching for him elsewhere. Denning, believing he had continued northward, would concentrate his efforts in that direction.

It did not matter. The important thing was that

he had thrown them off the trail. Now it was a question of quickly returning to the suffering Hob Lovan, getting him to where his wound could be properly treated — and then hurrying on to find Breckinridge.

Chapter Thirteen

It was full dark when John Mosby reached the thicket of scrub oak where Hob Lovan had taken refuge. He had used extreme care in returning. Although he was certain the Yankees were a considerable distance away from the immediate neighborhood, he left nothing to chance; Lovan's condition would not permit another wild and reckless flight across the countryside.

He halted at the edge of the thicket, listened into the night. He could hear nothing. After a time he rode deeper into the brush. Pausing when he judged he was somewhere near center, he gave the customary Ranger signal, the low, plaintive cry of a whippoorwill.

The reply came at once, and he moved toward the sound. It had arisen some distance ahead and to his left. He found Lovan in a shallow depression beneath a log. The scout had hidden his horse behind a clump of shaggy cedars off to one side.

"Right here, Major," he said as Mosby drew near. "You get rid of them Yanks?"

Mosby dismounted and hurried to where Lovan lay. "Last I saw of them they were riding north. Don't think they'll give us any more trouble."

At least for this night, he amended silently. Denning and Neill would not give up; they would continue to press the search.

"How's the leg?"

Lovan grunted as he drew himself out from under the log. "Sort of fixed it up myself while I was waitin'. I ain't bleedin' no more but I reckon I ought to get some medicine for it. Ain't got no hankerin' for gangrene."

Mosby nodded agreement in the darkness. There was little moon and the only light filtering down through the trees came from the stars.

"Can you ride?"

"Oh, sure. Can manage that all right. Where'll we go?"

"Find us a farmhouse somewhere close by. Get you fixed up."

"Be lucky if the danged Yankees ain't took 'em all over by now."

Mosby was silent for a few moments. Then, "We're a ways south of my usual stomping grounds and I don't know this area very well. You any suggestions?"

Lovan rubbed at his chin. "Yeh, reckon I do. Fact is I been layin' here thinkin' about it while you was takin' them Yanks on that snipe hunt. I figure we're a bit west of Culpepper town. Maybe a scant to the north. If I'm calculatin' right, we ought to be close to the Scott place."

"People you know?"

"Yep. Worked for Tom Scott a couple of times before the war. Fine folks. They'll give us some help if they're still around."

Mosby got to his feet, reached down for Lovan's hand and helped him to rise. "Good. That's just what we're looking for. A little attention to that leg of yours, a bite to eat, a couple of hours rest — and you'll be good as new."

Lovan glanced skeptically at the Ranger. "We ain't got time for all that, have we?"

"We're doing all right," Mosby replied. "Don't fret about it."

He helped the scout to his horse, assisted him onto the saddle. Lovan looked down at him.

"You could do with a bit of eatin' and sleepin' yourself," he observed.

Mosby moved off to where the bay waited. "For a fact," he said. He had paid little attention to his own needs up to that moment. Now it was hitting him all at once. Events had happened so rapidly since they departed the Confederate camp, less than twenty four hours previous, that there had been no time to think of anything except escape.

Lovan, sitting stiffly upright on his saddle, wheeled in beside him. "One thing we'd better be watchin' out for, Major," he said. "The Scotts got a mighty nice farm. Wouldn't surprise me none to find some Yankee gen'ral's moved in and took it over for his headquarters. We get there, we better ease around careful like 'til we know for sure what's what."

Mosby said, "You're right. Lead off, I'll follow."

They moved out into the starlight-dappled darkness, walking their horses slowly over the uneven ground. Mosby, fighting sleep and weariness, dozed in the saddle but never for periods longer than two or three minutes at a time. Hob Lovan seemed in much better condition than earlier. The hour's rest he had obtained while the Ranger was leading Jasper Denning and the Yankee sergeant off into the forest had benefited him greatly.

The night wore on. Somewhere near ten o'clock Lovan pulled to a stop. Mosby moved up beside the old scout, fearful that his wound had turned worse and that he was being compelled to halt. To his relief he discovered they had reached the Scott farm and were at the edge of its lower field. He could see the house, a large, two-storied affair with white fronting columns and many windows. It stood just beyond the expanse of cleared ground.

"We're here," Lovan said, shifting painfully on the black. He stared off into the night. "Don't see no signs of Yankees campin' about but I reckon we'd better go in careful."

"Let's drop back through the woods," Mosby said, looking closely at the scout. He was thankful they had no farther to travel. He doubted if Hob Lovan could continue any longer. "We ought to come in at the rear that way."

Lovan said, "Just what we'll do," and rode on.

The house was dark when they reached it. They drew to a halt behind the barn and Mosby, slipping from the bay, hurried off into the night to investigate. A single horse was in a rear stall. There were no signs of others having been there recently. He returned to Lovan, told him what he had found.

"That'll be Tom's," the scout said. "Had two

fine teams when I was here before. Except the army took them off'n his hands. Was just lookin' the house over. Appears mighty deserted. Yankees must have fair stripped old Tom.''

Mosby, still on foot and leading the bay, started forward. He motioned for Lovan to stay on the saddle. If they ran into Union soldiers quartered inside the structure there would be little time to escape. And Lovan, hampered by his wounded leg, would have great difficulty getting back onto the black.

They reached the house. Leaving the scout behind a clump of lilac, Mosby crept to the door. He tried it quietly, found it locked. He circled the structure, endeavored to peer through the windows. The shades were all drawn tightly. The side and front entrances he also found secured. When he returned to Lovan he was certain of only one thing; there were no soldiers nearby. Whether there was someone in the house he could only guess.

''Nothin' we can do but try knockin','' the scout said. ''Knowin' Tom Scott, I'd say he was inside. Doubt if the Yankees could scare him off his own property.''

Mosby, drawing one of his revolvers, stepped to the door. He rapped on it sharply. There was no response. He tried again, this time rattling the door noisily. Immediately a window overhead on the upper floor opened.

''Who's that? What do you want?'' a voice demanded.

The scout heaved a sigh, ''It's me — Hob Lovan, Tom. Me and Major Mosby. We're needin' help.''

There was a brief silence and then the window closed. Mosby heard the scuff of boots and shortly the door opened. A tall, angular man in a white nightshirt stood before them.

"Come in — come in quick!" he said urgently.

Mosby helped Lovan off his horse, then turned to tie the two animals to the lilac. He hurried back to the house. While Scott closed and barred the door and checked all the window shades, he helped Lovan into a chair. Scott finally lit the lamp.

The scout's face was ashen. His eyes were bright and mirrored the pain that slogged through him. Mosby squatted down beside him, examined the bullet wound hurriedly. He turned to Scott.

"Hob's been shot and we've had to ride a long way without doing anything for the wound. Can you get me some hot water and bandage? And something to disinfect with?"

Scott, his beard and mustache silver in the lamp-light, hesitated. "He say you were John Mosby?"

"Yes. We're on a mission for General Lee. Ran into a little trouble."

"Yankees?"

Mosby nodded impatiently at the question. "Yes," he said. There was no time to go into details over the incident. Hob's wound had actually been caused by one of Hunt's outlaws but that would require a lengthy, involved explanation. "How about it?"

Scott said, "All right," in an unenthusiastic way. "Those Yankees — they on your trail?"

"No, not now. We shook them off. You don't need to worry."

Scott shuffled off, taking the lamp with him. Mosby heard him moving about in the next room.

"Bring him in here," the farmer called after a few minutes.

Mosby slipped his arm around Lovan, half carried him through the doorway into what proved to be the kitchen. Scott had pulled on a pair of trousers over his nightshirt, was building a fire in the stove as they entered.

"Lay him over there on that cot," he said, pointing to a narrow bed against one wall. "I'll get the water to heating."

He disappeared into another part of the house, was back in only moments. He placed a bottle of medicine and a fold of cotton cloth on the table. Without looking at Mosby he said, "Water'll be ready pretty quick. You all hungry?"

Mosby said, "Yes, but that can wait. We've got to fix up Hob's leg."

"He'll be all right," Scott said. "Soon as we get that hole washed out and doctored. Had a little vittles left over from supper. I'll warm them. Guess a glass of brandy would feel right good, too."

Without waiting for Mosby to answer, Scott opened a cabinet and produced a bottle. He poured two tumblers well over half full, handed one to the Ranger chief. "Swallow this down, Major. I'll look after Hob."

The fiery liquor helped considerably. Mosby felt it slip through his body, dispelling some of the weariness, relaxing him, brightening his mind. Hob Lovan also began to revive. He stirred, glanced frowningly around the room. Finally, he focused his eyes on Mosby.

"Everythin' all right, Major?"

"Coming along fine. We'll have you fixed up first class in a few minutes."

Scott was placing food on the table. "Help yourself to this," he said. "Soon as that water's boiling, we'll have some tea."

He smiled faintly at Mosby. "Sorry if I was a little skittish at first there, Major. It ain't that I don't want to help. It's just that the way things are, I sure got to watch my step."

Mosby nodded his understanding. "There Yankees around here close?"

Scott straightened up. "You don't know?" he said in surprise. "Why, Major — you're right in the middle of a whole nest of them!"

Chapter Fourteen

John Mosby digested that bit of information slowly. "Figured there were a few scattered patrols still about but I thought most of the Union army was with Grant at Spottsylvania Court House."

"Not by a jug full!" Scott declared. "He's got reserves bivouacked all through here. Why, not five miles away they've even got a prison camp. Must be a good two thousand Confederate soldiers being held there."

The kettle of water began to rumble gently on the stove. Scott reached for it, poured the cups of tea, sloshed the balance into a wash basin. "You two go ahead with your eating and tea drinking," he said. "I'll look after the doctoring."

There were several minutes of quiet while the Rangers sipped slowly at their drinks and the farmer worked at Hob Lovan's wound.

"Where's the family?" the scout asked, finally. "You the only one on the place?"

Scott picked up the bottle of disinfectant, paused. "Had to send them off to Baltimore. Things too uncertain around here. Only reason I stayed was to protect my property, much as I could. This is going to burn like hades, Hob, but it's got to be done.''

Lovan took a deep swallow of the hot tea, drinking leaves and all. "Go ahead," he muttered.

The old scout writhed briefly as the medicine seared raw flesh but he uttered no sound. When it was over and Scott was wrapping a bandage about the leg, Mosby spoke.

"That prison camp — there much Union army there?''

Scott shook his head. "Maybe a couple of hundred men. They moved in and took over a little town — place we call Hazelville. It's sort of headquarters and a supply depot."

Hob Lovan, beginning to feel better after Scott's ministrations, abetted by the brandy, the food and the hot tea, lifted his eyes to Mosby. "You figurin' on somethin', Major?''

Mosby said, "No," in a quick, decisive way. "Was just wondering about it."

But he was thinking of two thousand Confederate soldiers being held prisoner only a short distance away; of Robert E. Lee's critical need for every man in the coming defense of Richmond. If they could somehow be freed to rejoin the Southern forces . . .

"What are you doing this far north?'' Scott asked. "Understood the Army of Northern Virginia was moving south."

"On a mission for the General," Lovan said. "He wants Breckinridge to . . .'' The scout caught Mosby's warning frown and checked his words.

Scott, finished with his medical chores, moved back to the stove. He refilled the kettle from a wooden water bucket, removed a lid from the top of the stove and set the utensil over the flames. "Be ready for more tea in a minute," he said. "You get enough to eat?"

Mosby nodded. Lovan yawned, said, "A-plenty, Tom. And we're obliged to you."

"You're welcome. How's the leg feel now?"

"Lots better."

The farmer began to collect the dishes. "Figures it would. That there stuff," he said, indicating the bottle of disinfectant, "is something my wife mixed up. Always does the job." He paused over the table. "Sounds like Lee's going to make a stand against Grant. Don't make sense to me. Be nothing but a terrible waste of men. From what I hear the war's about over."

"You've been listenin' to the wrong people," Lovan said drily. "We ain't about to call it quits."

Scott shrugged. "Be the best thing we could do. With the Union army getting bigger and stronger every day, and Lee getting weaker, what's the use of stringing it out?"

"General Lee is far from being defeated," Mosby said. "Grant will never take Richmond."

"Yankees seem to be doing a good job of pushing the whole Confederate army back toward it. I'm not so sure they won't finally win out."

"Nope, they'll never do it," Lovan said flatly. "You can bet your Sunday shoes on that."

"Well, I wish it would end," Scott said, sinking into a chair. "I'm sick and tired of it. Times are hard and getting harder — and for what? I worked like a slave to build myself a good farm, then along comes this war that don't mean a thing to me —

and I lose everything. All I got left is this house and what's in it. War took everything else; livestock, crops, money, even the grass in my pastures.''

"You're fortunate," Mosby said quietly. "Your house is still standing. Most places like this have been burned to the ground by the Yankees."

"So would this one if I hadn't stayed right here," Scott replied. "I set pat, got along with them, didn't give them no trouble . . ."

Mosby and Hob Lovan said nothing. The kettle murmured. The scout reached for it, silently refilled all the cups.

"Don't see anything wrong with what I done!" Scott said, defensively. "Wasn't hurting anybody, was just looking out for myself and what's mine. I ain't no traitor or anything like that."

"Man has a right to do what he thinks best," Mosby said. "And to his own opinions, as well. Maybe we don't agree with you, but that's one of the things we're fighting this war over — a man's right to do his own thinking and make his own decisions."

"Well, maybe so, but like I said, I wish it was all over — and it could be if Lee would only admit he's beat. Like most people, I'm fed up with it. It's done nothing for us but bring grief down on our heads and cost us all we own. Had my way," Scott added bitterly, "I'd call the thing off right this minute, bring an end to this killing and burning and such!"

Hob Lovan shook his head. "That day ain't likely to come soon, Tom. Not until we get a few things settled."

"You're just hoping. The Union will win this

war, you'll see. And then it will be worse than ever for us. Longer we keep on fighting them, harder it will be for us when it's finally over.''

"If we lose," Mosby said. "You're basing everything on a Yankee victory. I don't happen to believe it will turn out that way.''

Scott lifted his hands palms upward, allowed them to fall heavily. "Well, I ain't one to try and tell the devil how to run hell, but I sure don't see any sense in fighting now. We're licked and the sooner we admit it, the sooner we can settle down and start over. You say you're on your way to Breckinridge?''

Before Hob Lovan could answer Mosby said, "We're doing a bit of scouting, mostly.''

Scott rose to his feet. "Looks like you been going at it without much sleep. Bed there in the next room. You're welcome to use it.''

Mosby nodded. Rest would do both Lovan and himself a world of good. It would particularly benefit the scout and his wounded leg, and they would need to be at their best and on full alert when they resumed their journey if, as Scott had said, the country was overrun with Yankees.

"Again we're obliged to you," he said. "We can use three or four hours' sleep.''

Tom Scott stretched, yawned. "Fine. You go ahead. I'll use the cot there.''

"We'll need to be up and on our way an hour or so before daylight," Mosby said.

"I'll wake you. Expect I'd better go look after your horses. Don't want them standing out there in the open where they could be seen. I'll put them in the barn. Ought to be a little hay left.''

Mosby and Lovan got to their feet, moved toward the adjoining bedroom. The scout walked stiffly but without too much pain and effort. Scott followed them to the doorway and halted. He watched them lie down.

"Don't worry none about oversleeping," he said. "I'll get you up in plenty of time."

He smiled and turned away. Mosby heard him cross the room and open the back door. The Ranger chief was not entirely at ease. Something disturbed him vaguely but he could not put his finger on the exact cause. He turned to say something to Lovan but the scout was already asleep, snoring faintly in his near exhaustion. Mosby drew himself to the edge of the bed and arose. He walked to the window, carefully drew aside the shade and looked out.

Scott was leading their two horses toward the barn. He reached the structure, disappeared into its dark interior. He was there for several long minutes, then emerged, started for the house in slow, lengthy strides.

Mosby returned to his place on the bed. He guessed he was simply tired, that it was making him overly suspicious. Tom Scott was all right. There was no danger. He closed his eyes, dozed off . . .

Chapter Fifteen

John Mosby awoke with a start. The room, with the shades tightly drawn over the windows, was still pitch dark but he had a feeling that sunrise was not far off. He listened, wondering what it had been that aroused him. The house lay in silence, the only sound the rasp of Hob Lovan's breathing.

The Ranger slipped off the bed quietly, moved to the doorway and glanced into the kitchen. There was no sign of Tom Scott and the cot was as Lovan had left it. Alarm began to flow through Mosby. He crossed the room in three steps, drew back the window covering. It was daylight. Dawn could be only minutes away. He wheeled swiftly, returned to where Lovan lay sleeping. He shook the scout awake.

"Something's wrong! We've got to get out of here!"

Lovan scrambled to his feet, forgetting his injured leg. He throttled the gasp of pain that sprang to his lips. "What is it? What's wrong?"

Mosby was already moving for the rear door. "It's almost sunrise — and Scott's not around."

Lovan, hurrying in a stiff, awkward way, followed. "Said he'd call us. Reckon he overslept hisself."

Mosby opened the door cautiously, glanced about. The yard was empty, quiet. "Don't think he's even on the place. And he never used that cot like he planned. Can you walk?"

"Most good as new," the scout answered.

"Let's get to the horses. Won't feel right until we're out of here and in the brush."

Mosby headed for the barn at a fast pace, Lovan, favoring his leg, keeping up with him nevertheless. They reached the structure and pulled back the door. A sigh slipped from the Ranger chief's lips. Their horses were still in their stalls. He had been afraid . . .

"You say Tom had a horse in here when we rode up last night?" Lovan asked.

Mosby came to sudden attention. "He did. In that last stall."

"Ain't none there now," the scout said, leading his mount toward the door. "You're guessin' right, Major. There sure is somethin' goin' on around here and it don't smell good."

They led their horses into the yard and swung to the saddle. Lovan had a small difficulty finding a comfortable position for his injured leg but he made no comment. They wheeled about and circled the barn, angling immediately for the thick brush on the far side of the clearing.

Once they gained that shelter Lovan pushed up beside Mosby. "Was just thinkin', Scott could have gone out on some errard, maybe after grub . . ."

Mosby shook his head. "He knew we had to be

up and on the move early. Promised to call us. There's some other reason, Hob.''

"Could've slipped his mind.''

"Maybe, but I doubt it. However, if I'm too suspicious and made a mistake about the man, I'll apologize next time we see him. Until then I prefer to play it safe.''

"Horses comin','' Lovan warned suddenly, pulling to a stop.

Mosby caught the sound and together the two Rangers wheeled off into a prickly stand of wild roses. There were several riders, coming from the west and headed toward the Scott place.

Deep in the screening foliage Mosby and Hob Lovan waited. The horsemen broke into view, riding two abreast along the well beaten trail. There were eight men in all, and as they curved into sight the Confederates saw the man beside the sergeant in the lead was Tom Scott.

Hob Lovan choked on a curse. "That damn traitor!'' he managed. "Bedded us down, then went after the Yankees. If I wasn't seein' it with my own eyes, I'd never believe it.''

"Must have made up his mind to do it after we went to sleep,'' Mosby said.

"A damn traitor,'' the scout said again, repeating himself. "A lousy turncoat. He's worse'n Denning and his crowd!''

"Don't be too hard on him,'' Mosby said, watching the patrol trot by. "He honestly thinks he's doing the right thing. And down in his heart I doubt if he really is a traitor. He's just so worked up over the trouble and hardship the war has heaped on him that he'll do anything to end it.''

"Could have got us both hung, that kind of thinkin'."

"Probably didn't consider that part of it. He figures if we're caught and Breckinridge doesn't get Lee's message, or whatever it is we're going to him about, it will help matters along."

"Still a damn traitor, far as I'm concerned," the scout muttered in a low voice. "And if I ever get the chance I'm tellin' him so . . ."

"Add a few words for me," Mosby said. "For a while back at his place this morning I thought we were in for it again. But it's done with now. We've given them the slip. Which way is Hazelville from here?"

Lovan glanced at Mosby, his eyes sharp and bright. "Hazelville — where them prisoners are? Then you've got somethin' cookin' in your mind?"

Mosby said, "Yes. Like to look things over. General Lee could certainly use two thousand more men."

Lovan smiled broadly. "Sure good to see you figurin' things like that again, Major! Had me worried there for a spell, way you was actin' after you heard about General Jeb. Thought you was about to give up. But Hazelville — last night you said . . ."

"Just didn't want to do any talking around Scott. He sounded a little off key to me at the start and I don't like to run chances."

Lovan bobbed his head ruefully. "I thought old Tom was all right, but I guess I'll learn one of these days to keep my yap shut, too. Scott wouldn't have knowed nothin' if I hadn't a spoke out of turn."

"No real harm done," Mosby said. "Far as Breckinridge is concerned, the Yankee generals know all about it anyway. Denning saw to that. What about Hazelville?''

Lovan squinted toward the east, lightening now with the sun's first rays. ''All we got to do is bear due west and we'll hit it. You figure we got the time to spare? Hadn't we better keep headin' for the Shenandoah?''

''Sooner we get there the better, of course. But this won't be any out of our way, and if there's a chance we can help those prisoners escape, even a part of them, we're duty bound to try.''

Lovan said, ''Sure, you're right,'' and put his horse into motion.

They rode on with the rising sun to their backs, always keeping in the brush and avoiding the trails and rutted roads. They were in country thick with Yankees and several times they saw patrols in the distance but always in time to avoid being noticed.

Thinking of this John Mosby wondered if it would be wise to forget Hazelville after all, swing by it in a wide circle and side-step the possibility of trouble. Should both he and Lovan be captured by Union soldiers, Lee's message would never reach Breckinridge — and the reinforcements the Confederate leader needed so badly would not arrive. Such could turn the tide strongly in Grant's favor.

But the risk was worth it. And if they were careful and could rely on just a small amount of luck, they would avoid capture. One of them would get through, Mosby thought, and then made a silent vow; if they made an attempt at Hazelville to free the prisoners and it came to grief, he would see to it, at any cost, that Hob Lovan escaped to carry Lee's message on to the Shenandoah.

Lovan pulled to a halt a dozen paces ahead and pointed to a streak of smoke trickling into the morning sky beyond a hill before them.

"That'll be the town," he said.

Mosby stared at the smoke for a minute. "What's the country like around it? Any way to get in close without being spotted?"

"Town's in a little valley," the scout answered. "Hills all around it but they've been cleared of timber. If we cut around to the south, howsomever, we can follow the creek in. "It's really brushy."

Mosby said, "That's the way we'll go."

They swung off, completely circled the hill and entered the valley at its lower end. A small stream flowed along the floor of the swale and, as Lovan said, it was heavily overgrown with berry bushes, sassafras, hemlock and similar trees and shrubbery.

They began to hear sounds of activities long before the village came into view; the ring of an anvil as a blacksmith plied his trade, the barking of a dog, the voice of a man singing in a high tenor voice. Somewhere a carpenter rapped with steady beat as he hammered something together.

"You say this creek goes clear through town?"

Lovan said, "Sure does, Major. Runs along the back side, maybe twenty-thirty yards from the houses."

Mosby nodded thoughtfully. Then, "Guess we first better get a look at the place. Want to see where they've put all those prisoners."

Lovan pointed toward the hillside to their right. "Brush runs up there for a piece. We can climb up and nobody'll see us while we're doin' it."

They veered off, rode a short distance up the

slope. Where the brush ended they halted and dismounted. Mosby, with Lovan hobbling along at his side, walked to the fringe of the shrubbery.

"There she is," the scout said, waving his hand at the scatter of houses and small buildings.

Hazelville wasn't much, Mosby saw — a dozen or less residences, four or five business structures. All lay in the exact center of the bowl with the stream, as Lovan had said, cutting a path at the lower side. He located the prison compound, scarcely more than a field around which wire and logs had been laid to form a square. Evidently it was a temporary camp; the prisoners were probably en route to some major point.

"Sure don't see many Yankees," Lovan commented. "I figured this here place would be crawlin' with 'em."

There appeared to be sentries placed around the stockade every thirty or forty feet, Mosby noted. They would be well armed; still, if a determined effort were made, it seemed an escape would be possible.

He saw the cannon then.

They had been drawn up on the slope overlooking the stockade — five Napoleon guns placed in a semicircle and pointed down into the prison camp. They would be loaded with cannister, Mosby guessed, which explained why a company of Yankees could control so many prisoners.

At the first sign of trouble the gun crews stationed behind the cannon would leap to their positions and open up on the Confederates with a hail of deadly shrapnel. The crews likely were on duty around the clock. Headquarters for the Union force would be the field of white tents just beyond and to the left of the town.

Hob Lovan clawed at his beard. "Sure don't see how we can do much for them boys. First place, how we ever goin' to get in close? And if we did, what about them cannons?"

John Mosby brought his attention back to the village itself. "Only one answer to that — to both questions. We've got to make the Yankees look the other way."

Chapter Sixteen

"Now, just how in tarnation you figure to do that?" Hob Lovan demanded. He pulled himself about, shifted his weight to relieve his injured leg. "And if we can make them Yanks look the other way, won't be long enough for us to do anythin'."

Mosby said, "Maybe. Scott told us the army was using the town for headquarters. That means it will also be a supply depot. Those buildings down there will have been commandeered for storage — and one of them, maybe more, will have munitions — gunpowder and such stacked inside it. If a man were to get down there, start a fire . . ."

"And set that ammunition to blowin'," Lovan added, his face brightening, "all them soldiers would hightail it for town to help . . ." The scout paused, glanced toward the cannon. "Exceptin' maybe them gun crews. Doubt if they'd leave. Be their job to keep the prisoners pinned down."

"I'd figure it that way," the Ranger chief said.

"Then how we goin' to get all them boys out of the stockade without all of us gettin' a hide full of cannister? Five cannon sure can throw a whale of a lot of iron!"

"True, but if a man circled that hill and came in behind the guns — the end one, he'd probably have a chance to move in fast and take over when the excitement started. The crews would be looking the other way and since those guns are on wheels, be no big job to wheel one around and cover all the rest."

Hob Lovan was grinning again. "Sure would work, 'specially if some of them Yankee gunners run over to the edge of the hill where they could see the town better."

"Even if they didn't and they all stayed at their posts, which is doubtful, it should be possible for a man to take over during the excitement — one gun, at least."

"What about the guards they got spotted around the stockade?"

"I'll take care of them," Mosby said.

The scout's grin broadened. "Then I'm goin' up after the cannon, that it?"

Mosby nodded. "Here's what I've got in mind. We'll have to move careful since we can't wait until dark. You swing back up on the hill and get behind the cannons. Watch out for Yankee patrols. They'll be all around here. I'll get into town by following the creek. Probably take me a bit more time than you because I've got to locate the building where they've got the ammunition stored. Don't get jumpy if you don't hear from me right away.

"Signal for you to move in and grab one of the

cannons will be when the explosion goes off and the gun crews leave their posts.''

''Where'll you be?''

''Soon as I get a fire started and am certain the ammunition will blow, I'll double back to the stockade. I'll have to get by those sentries and let the prisoners know what's happening so they can get out and make a run for the woods.''

Lovan's face clouded. He shook his head doubtfully. ''Don't know, Major. That's a lot of gettin' back and forth. Somethin' could go wrong mighty easy for you.''

''I know that, but for two thousand men it's worth the gamble. However, it's still secondary to the job of getting through to Breckinridge. No matter how it turns out, one of us must make it to the Shenandoah. Now, listen closely, Hob. I want you to understand this. When you're up on that hill and the ammunition depot blows up — if the Yankees don't do what I've figured they would, don't try to take over the cannon. Just forget it. Get on your horse and head out. Is that clear?''

''Sure, Major. What about you?''

''I'll make a run for it from the other end of town. One of us will get through — maybe both.''

''You'll have a powerful lot of bluebellies on your neck down there.''

''Won't be the first time. You got everything straight now?''

''Right down to a frog's hair,'' Lovan said. ''When do we start?''

''Now,'' Mosby said and extended his hand. ''Good luck, Hob.''

''Same to you, Major,'' the scout replied, moving toward his horse. "Meet you on the other side of the hill."

John Mosby remained motionless, his glance again on the settlement. He could see more soldiers now. And at the far end of the houses there was a work party doing repairs on a bridge that spanned the creek. He could not see the Union encampment too well, it being partially hidden by the rows of houses and buildings. Most of the soldiers would be there, he guessed. Only those assigned to specific duties, such as the gun crews, the sentries and the like would not be around the tents.

He turned then to the bay, swung onto the saddle. It was a daring plan he had concocted, fraught, as Hob Lovan had noted, with many pitfalls. But by its very daring it could succeed — and for two thousand men capable of fighting, of bolstering Lee's beleaguered army, the risk was justifiable and worthwhile.

He rode off into the brush that bound the creek, walking his horse slowly and quietly. It would not be an easy chore getting into town unseen. He had debated with himself the possibility of going on foot, decided it would appear more normal to a casual observer if he were seen on horseback. He could easily be taken for one of the neighboring farmers coming into the town for some purpose. Besides, he would need to return to the stockade as fast as possible once the fires were started. On a horse he could cover the distance quickly.

He gained the edge of the settlement without incident. The single street appeared to be deserted of civilians and he guessed the Union army had pretty well taken over the entire town with the exception of the residences themselves. There were a dozen or more blue-uniformed men standing about, most of them in front of a tavern.

Mosby began to search for the building he thought would be serving as a storehouse for the ammunition. There were only three fairly large structures in the settlement. The first in line was across the street. If it proved to be the one he sought he would have difficulty getting to it.

The second building, standing on the near side, appeared to have once been a livery barn. He dismounted, left the bay in the brush and started toward it over the uneven, open ground that lay between the creek and the village, walking in slow, easy strides.

Although he was shut off from the street by the building itself, he felt his nerves singing, his muscles tightening with tension. It seemed a dozen pairs of eyes must be upon him and at every step he half expected someone to sing out, to challenge him. But he reached the rear of the barn without interruption.

He paused there, impatiently brushed the beads of sweat from his forehead, and then moved to the door. It was nailed shut. Smothering his disappointment he continued on to a window and peered through its dust-streaked glass. At the opposite end of the structure he could see a square of light. A doorway — with three soldiers standing within it.

The barn was filled with boxes, crates, and other items. He could see stacks of saddles, several rows of team harness. A mound of canvas feed bags filled one corner and directly to his right there were two newly painted ambulances. He pulled back. This was part of the Yankee supply depot but it contained no ammunition. Gunpowder, shells, muskets and the like would be in a building to themselves.

Before he continued, he thought of returning to the stream and getting his horse. If the depot proved to be at the far end of the village, he would be a considerable distance from the bay when the moment came to flee. But he decided it was still wise to leave the animal where he stood. Crossing and recrossing the cleared ground was dangerous, and it was foolhardy to press his luck. He moved on, keeping close to the sheds and houses, taking advantage of every bit of cover yet striving to not appear obvious.

The next building was smaller than the first, and constructed of field stone. Once it could have been the town hall, or perhaps the schoolhouse. It stood slightly back from the street and Mosby had no difficulty approaching it from the rear. There was but a single window in the wall and it, he saw, was barred. He looked into it and a quick surge of excitement raced through him. It was the ammunition storeroom.

Standing deep in a clump of wild plum bushes that grew close to the building, Mosby raked his mind for a means of gaining entrance. There was but one door, and it faced the street. Even if he dared show himself, he knew he would find it securely locked.

He turned to the window. The sash lifted easily, caught on its spring pegs and remained up. Mosby tugged at the bars. They were rigid, deeply imbedded in the mortar above and below the opening. They were six inches or less apart, scarcely wide enough for a man to thrust his arm between.

Now he had a better view of the storehouse interior. Along one wall there were several dozen kegs of gunpowder, all tightly sealed. Down the center of the room were boxes of pistols, muskets and other weapons. To his right there was a row of small, white muslin sacks all solidly packed and tied neatly at one end with cord.

Powder charges!

Hope lifted within the Ranger. If he could manage to ignite one of the sacks, so tightly filled with gunpowder, he would not have to risk the use of fire and the possibility of its being noticed and extinguished before the damage could be done. The gunpowder would go quickly, would set off the kegs and the entire depot would blow up fast.

But how to ignite one of the sacks — one was all it would take — was the problem. He considered setting fire to a handful of brush, tossing it against the row of sacks. One might catch but it was a remote chance, and again there was the risk of discovery. The smoke from the burning brush might attract a passer-by, or one of the soldiers idling about the street before the flames could do their work.

His knife . . .

The solution came to him suddenly. He stooped, drew the blade from its sheath inside his boot. Expert, as were all Rangers, he could throw it with deadly accuracy. And this, not being a moving target, would be simple. All he need do was hurl it hard enough to split open one of the sacks of powder, allow a quantity of it to spill down onto the floor.

Now that the plan was devised, he turned, made a careful survey of his surroundings. No one had appeared in the narrow strip of cleared land that separated the village from the creek. He located the bay, barely visible in the brush fifty yards away, and chose the path he would take to reach him. That all clear in his mind, he bent down, gathered up a handful of dry leaves and twigs and fashioned a simple torch, binding it together with a bit of vine. He then resumed his post at the window.

He took his knife in hand, started to thrust his arm between the bars, prepared for the throw. He heard a noise at the door, the loud rattle of chain. Instantly he drew back, dropped to his knees. Someone was entering the building. If they noticed the open window . . .

He listened, waited, scarcely breathing. He heard a voice speak.

"How many?"

"Twenty-four," came a reply. "For them new recruits that come in this mornin'."

There was silence after that. Mosby wondered: Were they doing something — or had they noticed the window and were considering it, possibly at that very moment working their way around the building to investigate? He laid his improvised torch on the ground and drew one of his revolvers. If they appeared he would be forced to shoot. And then he would do his best to set off the gunpowder. He might as well do as much damage to the Yankees as possible.

"All right, Sergeant. I got 'em."

Mosby drew a long breath. He heard the door slam, again caught the rattle of chain. He remained crouched for several minutes, allowing ample time, and then raised himself to the edge of the window and looked in. The Yankees had gone.

Again taking the knife by the point, he pushed his arm through the bars. By moving his body to one side he found he had a clean, easy throw at the powder sacks. He chose one near the center of the stack, and in the second row above the floor. The brief moment that would elapse when the powder caught fire and leaped to the open sack would give him time enough to heave himself back from the window, and possibly avoid the initial blast.

He must be accurate. He must strike the bag, knife point first and with sufficient force to slice open the cloth. He would get no second chance.

Mosby set himself squarely, balanced the razor-edged weapon between his fingers. He made two preliminary false throws, getting the feel of his position. The window bars cramped his movements to some degree but it was no serious problem.

Suddenly his arm whipped downward. The knife flashed through the air, struck the sack with a dull thud. It plunged in half the blade deep — and hung there. Dismay settled over Mosby. The blade had ripped into the sack but the tough cloth held it in place. The hole remained plugged.

He pulled back, looked about for a stone or some such object to throw at the knife and dislodge it. He heard a faint sound, looked quickly into the room. The knife had fallen to the floor. A steady stream of powder was cascading from the opening in the muslin and was building a small pyramid at the base of the row.

Mosby drew a match from his pocket, scratched

it into flame. He held it to the torch until the twigs and leaves burned steadily, and then returned to the window. He paused. Now was the critical moment. He must take care to toss the burning twigs accurately, yet he must have time to get clear of the building or else be trapped by the explosion that would follow.

The gunpowder was still flowing from the punctured sack, was now a two-inch-high pile. Mosby fixed the center of the stack above it as his target. He would gain a precious second or two by throwing the torch high, allowing it to drop onto the explosive.

He twisted himself around, prepared to make the dash for the creek and his waiting horse the instant the torch left his fingers. He took a final glance at the small bundle of flames. It was burning strongly. There was no possibility of its being snuffed out upon impact. He drew a deep breath, made a final survey of the cleared ground to be certain he was not being watched. All was clear.

He raised his arm, threw the knot of flaming trash at the row of sacks — and leaped away.

Chapter Seventeen

"Fire!"

The cry caught John Mosby before he had covered a half dozen frantic steps. It came from the street, from in front of the building. Someone had been standing close by, had seen the arcing torch. It was sheer luck — but there was no need for alarm on the Ranger's part. It was too late for the Yankees to do anything about it now.

"Fire! In the pow . . ."

The building rocked with an explosion. Glass shattered and a billowing cloud of smoke belched from the window. A long tongue of flame lashed out, licked hungrily at the world beyond the walls. Mosby felt a hot blast of air strike him, but he kept his feet, raced on for the brush. This was only the beginning — the first touch of fire to the spilling gunpowder. The major explosion was yet to be — just seconds away.

It came with a mighty roar and a tremendous upheaval of wind. Mosby, only a yard from the sheltering brush along the creek, felt himself flung forward. There was a blinding flash. The building seemed to come apart in all directions and the air was suddenly filled with bits of rock, wood, dust and mortar. Mosby, on his hands and knees, scrambled to get into the shrubbery. He felt the scorching breath of the explosion touch him, felt also the pelting of the debris as it began to rain down.

But he was unhurt. He leaped to his feet, raced to where the nervously shying bay awaited him. He vaulted to the saddle, jerked the reins free and wheeled about. He spurred off, riding recklessly, heedlessly, dodging in and out of the trees and shrubs. He could hear men shouting. Abruptly there was another earthshaking explosion.

That would be the kegs of gunpowder starting to go up. He flung a glance over his shoulder. He could see the street now. Soldiers were streaming down from the camp, converging from all other parts of the town. The building was a seething inferno shooting up rockets of fire that were falling on other structures, igniting new pockets of flame.

Mosby rushed on. He drew near the stockade, looked toward the cannon on the hill. Two of the gun crews had deserted their positions, were trotting toward the roaring conflagration. The remaining three had drawn forward of their posts, were watching intently. There was no sign of Hob Lovan.

He drew abreast the stockade. He could see the Confederate prisoners all gathered at the lower end. They were shouting and cheering. The sentries stationed around the field were standing firm.

He rode on until he was directly opposite the far corner of the enclosed field. He leaped from the saddle, hastily secured the bay and hurried through the brush. He halted at the edge of the growth. The nearest sentry, his back turned to Mosby, was a dozen yards away. Mosby drew his revolver. He took it by the barrel, intending to use it as a club. A gunshot would draw the attention of the others. He slipped up to the man silently, felled him with a sharp blow to the head.

At that moment a cannon roared through the confusion of sounds. Mosby glanced toward the slope. Lovan had wheeled one of the guns about, trained it on the other four and fired it. Three of the weapons had been overturned by the blast and were now disabled. As Mosby watched the scout, running in a peculiar, hobbled manner, was making it to the one remaining field gun. The crew, caught off guard and thoroughly amazed, were staring at him as though mesmerized.

Mosby leaped over the fallen Yankee and ran for the stockade fence. He saw the sentry to his left spin and look blankly at him. The soldier then noted his sprawling comrade. It jarred him to reality. He threw up his musket, prepared to shoot. Mosby fired two quick bullets at the man and saw him fall.

The fire and explosions at the far end of town were increasing, filling the air with a steady booming and crackling. It was doubtful if the soldiers in that area had even noted the report of the cannon Lovan had set off. If so, they were ignoring it and were concentrating on the supply depot.

Mosby glanced again to the slope. Lovan was in possession of the second gun. He had it pointed toward the gun crews who were giving way, falling back toward town. Hob Lovan was in complete command of the hill.

The Ranger chief reached the stockade fence, went over it in a long jump, and rushed on for the mass of milling Confederate prisoners. Many of them had turned, had seen him and were advancing in his direction. He could not see the rest of the Yankee sentries. They had disappeared.

Three young Confederates, their faces bright with excitement, were the first to meet him.

"What's going on? What's happening?" one yelled.

"Get out of here!" Mosby replied. "You're free! Head south for Richmond!"

"Prison break!" the second of the trio shouted, turning to face the crowd. "Come on — let's go!"

They raced by Mosby, leaping the fence and running hard for the cover of the brush along the creek. One stooped to retrieve the musket of the dead sentry and hurried on.

Men surged all around John Mosby now, yelling questions. An officer wearing the insignia of a colonel shouldered his way to the Ranger.

"What is this?" he demanded.

"Your chance to break out of here and rejoin General Lee at Richmond, Colonel," Mosby replied. "Get your men organized and away as fast as possible."

The officer frowned. "Rejoin Lee? That's impossible! And if we could — there's no point . . ."

"The Army of Northern Virginia will be making a stand against Grant in a few days. Somewhere near Richmond. Lee needs every available soldier!"

The officer drew himself up stiffly. "I'll be no party to prolonging a hopeless struggle . . ."

Mosby wheeled away angrily. He climbed onto a stump, raised his hands.

"Men! Listen to me! I'm John Mosby of the Confederate Rangers. Get out of here — head south for Richmond. General Lee is making a stand against Grant. He needs every one of you. Hurry — before the Yankees recover here and move in on you!"

Cheers drowned out Mosby's final words. The crowd swept past him toward the stockade fence. Some leaped over it but the majority simply flowed into it, trampled it underfoot in a tattered, irresistible flood. Once beyond the barrier they began to break up, separate into small groups, all moving into the brush and striking southward.

Mosby looked back, his eyes searching for the officer. The colonel was now leaving, being carried on with the others, caught up in the rush and unable to hold back even if he desired. He saw Mosby watching, looked away quickly. The Ranger shook his head. It was the second time in recent hours he had encountered a Confederate who was convinced the war was lost, that there was no use in further fighting.

He turned then, ran to his horse. His job was done. Some of the prisoners, probably most of them, would reach Richmond, rejoin Lee. Others would be recaptured trying to get through, while a few, such as the colonel, would make no attempt to fulfill their obligations. But the net result would be good. Lee and the army would benefit considerably.

He mounted the bay and swung across the valley. He started up the long slope toward Hob Lovan who still stood beside his cannon. They must pull out immediately. The Yankees would recover quickly from their initial shock, would come storming after the men who had perpetrated the outrage with vengeance in their hearts. Moreover, the explosions and smoke would have been noted by other outlying camps and patrols; the valley would soon be thick with soldiers.

He topped out the small rise that blocked his view of Lovan and saw the scout crouched beside the Napoleon. Lovan was looking down into the town where fire now raged in several buildings. Hazelville was doomed — and the name of John Mosby would be a hated one among civilians from that hour on, he realized. But it could not be helped. The result certainly justified the means.

He shifted his attention to the settlement, wondering what was drawing the old scout's consideration. A half hundred blue-clad soldiers were advancing down the street at a brisk trot. That explained what had happened to the sentries who had been scattered around the stockade; they had gone for reinforcements. Mosby spurred the bay onward, rushed to the side of Lovan.

As he came up the scout struck a match to a long taper, held it poised near the cannon. He had wheeled the gun about to where its gaping mouth had covered the street below. He was waiting for the moment when the charging Yankees would be in line with the muzzle.

Just as Mosby halted, Hob Lovan acted. The gun belched, leaped backwards on its wheels. A shrill whistling filled the air as the shot screamed toward the soldiers. A mighty churning of dust erupted in the street. A chorus of faint yells lifted, sounding distant and hollow. A dozen men writhed in the dirt while the remainder of the company scattered for cover behind nearby trees and shrubs.

"Come on!" Mosby shouted at the elated scout. "We've got to get clear of here!"

Lovan wheeled, came limping toward the Ranger chief. "Sure give them a dose of their own medicine!" he chortled. "Know what they was loadin' them cannon with? Rocks, nails, bits of scrap iron, pieces of wire. Anything they could find. Reckon they know now what it feels like!"

Mosby glanced anxiously toward the town. "Where's your horse?"

"Yonder side of the ridge."

"Get up behind me," Mosby ordered, spurring in close. "Expect we're going to have plenty of company."

"You can bet on that," the scout replied, pulling himself onto the bay. "We stirred up enough commotion to be heard in Washington!"

The bay started for the crest of the hill. Lovan was still talking. "Sure pulled that one off, didn't we, Major? Wrecked a whole blasted Yankee town — and set our boys loose. Can't ask for better luck than that!"

They gained the ridge, slanted down the opposite slope. Mosby saw Lovan's horse, tied to a stump fifty feet or so distant. He was glad the black was no farther away.

"Couldn't have worked out better," he admitted, replying to Lovan. "Now if that luck will just hold for another . . ."

"Which it sure won't," the scout broke in softly. "Over to the left, Major — Yankee cavalry!"

Chapter Eighteen

Mosby swiveled his glance to the side. Seven riders — Denning — the Yankee sergeant, Neill — and five more cavalrymen. Apparently they had been searching for Lovan and him, had heard the explosion in the town or seen the smoke and had hurried back to investigate.

The Ranger dug his heels into the bay, rushed toward Lovan's waiting mount. The scout hit the ground, went to one knee as his weak leg gave out. He was up instantly and leaping into the saddle.

Neill yelled something and the cavalry patrol began to curve about and swing in. Mosby, with Lovan only a breath behind, spun around and started down the long slope. There was no other choice. The Yankees had cut off the route to the west, toward Massanutten Mountain and New Market.

But ahead lay trouble. The Union force in Hazelville, smarting under their losses not only by fire but of their prisoners as well, and no longer intimidated by Lovan and the cannon he had captured, were swarming up the hill.

Trapped between the two groups, Mosby wheeled left, drove hard along the crest of the ridge. Such course would take them straight into the Yankee camp lying just west of the village. But again there was no alternative; and he was gambling — gambling that most of the Yankee soldiers were either down in the settlement battling the spreading flames or else among those charging up the slope.

"Keep low!" he shouted back to Lovan. "We're going through the camp!"

Guns began to hammer as they plunged down the long grade. The shooting came from Denning and his cavalrymen, but the balls were wild, most of them high. Mosby could hear yelling on the slope now. He threw a glance to the ridge. Denning and Neill, riding side by side, were little more than a hundred yards away. The men on the hillside were not visible. A bulge on the face of the slope shut them off temporarily.

Slightly ahead of Lovan, he thundered into the cluster of tents, followed the narrow street that separated the center rows. He looked ahead, beyond the camp. There was nothing but open ground. The only cover available was along the creek, on the floor of the valley; they must reach it soon . . .

Two soldiers stepped into the roadway suddenly. They came from one of the larger tents. They were cooks, Mosby saw from their dress, and both held muskets. He drew his pistol, snapped a shot at the nearest, missed clean.

"Mosby!"

The man yelled the name and fired point-blank. The Ranger heard the ball whine by his head. He fired a second shot, saw the cook stagger and fall. Hob Lovan began to shoot but the second Yankee stood resolute, his musket leveled. Mosby saw the puff of smoke as he squeezed off his shot. At the same instant he felt the bay wilt under him and start to fall.

He kicked his feet out of the stirrups and jumped. He struck the ground solidly with the yells of Denning's cavalrymen ringing in his ears. He went down full length, rolled, bounded to his feet with the quick grace of a cat. He spun about. The cook lay prone, victim of Hob Lovan's revolver. He was only a step away from the first man. Denning and the others were surging in fast. Mosby drew his other pistol, threw two quick shots at them. A yell went up. The patrol began to break apart, wheel aside.

"Major — here!"

Lovan had wheeled, had come racing back, the flying hoofs of the black kicking down several tents as he cut in short. The scout veered in close, held out his hand. Mosby caught it, catapulted up behind him and they rushed on.

"Head for the brush — the creek!" Mosby cried in Lovan's ear. "Our only chance!"

He twisted about, faced Denning and Neill, and the Yankee cavalrymen. They had regrouped, were again coming on. But they no longer were in tight, compact order; now they were scattered. Mosby opened up with both guns, making little effort to take aim from his position on the galloping black. He could only shoot, hoping some of his bullets found a mark.

The Yankees again faltered in the face of his

blistering fire. The last of the tents fled by. Mosby felt the horse swerve and start down grade as Lovan pointed him toward the stream. They were a good quarter mile below the burning town, but smoke lay thick on the morning air and the crackling of the flames was loud.

They reached the bottom of the swale, streaked across the even ground, the dusty road used by freighters, and gained the fringe of brush. The shrubbery was heavier here, the creek much wider. Apparently it was used as a watering place for stock.

"Go left!" Mosby howled at Lovan.

The scout obediently angled the laboring horse to the north. They splashed through the shallow pond, the black's hooves sending sheets of water spraying out ahead. They raced on through the bushes, the small trees, the looping tangles of vines. Mosby, listening hard, could hear Denning and the others pounding across the open ground, crossing the road. The Yankees were shortening the gap.

"Keep going!" Mosby shouted at Lovan. "I'll find a horse — meet you at Thornton's Gap."

"Where'll you get . . ." Lovan began, half turning his head.

"I'll find one," the Ranger chief said, pushing himself farther back on the black's rump. "If I don't show at the Gap by sundown — ride on to Breckinridge."

Lovan wagged his head in protest. "Be better if we . . ."

Mosby threw himself clear of Lovan's horse. He hit the ground at an awkward angle, crashed full tilt into a clump of bushes. Pain shot through his left shoulder and lights momentarily popped before his eyes as his head came into sudden, violent contact with something solid. But he was up in only seconds, shaking himself to throw off the cobwebs. He could hear the Yankees rushing into the brush. They were dangerously close. If he had not leaped from Lovan's horse and thus relieved the animal of its extra burden, they would have been overtaken soon.

"There they go!"

Neill's voice was shrill, no more than a dozen yards away. Mosby, crouched behind a clump of blackberries, watched them pour into the shadowy brush and wheel left. The sergeant was in the lead now, followed closely by Denning and then the cavalrymen.

"Only one on that horse!" There was surprise in the voice.

"One of 'em's jumped off!"

Mosby listened to the cries. They had noted his absence sooner than he had anticipated. He had hoped the dense shrubbery would hide the fact from them for at least another mile.

"It's Mosby — he's gone!" Neill yelled.

"Hold up!" Denning's voice was more normal. "Couple of you keep on after the old man. Rest of you right wheel, follow me!"

The lieutenant was taking charge again. Mosby pulled away from the berry bushes, began to run toward the village. His best chance for obtaining a horse lay there. If he could get his hands on one, he could keep Denning and his crowd occupied, allow Lovan to escape and reach New Market. With only two cavalrymen on his trail the old scout would find it easy to elude his pursuers.

He heard the thrashing of brush as Denning and the men who still rode with him turned about, started back up the stream. It would be difficult to keep out of sight, particularly if they spread out. The band of shrubbery, while dense, was not wide. Four or five men advancing in a line could sweep it clean.

Mosby, keeping low, crossed to the extreme far edge. The best possibility of going unnoticed lay there. The trees were somewhat larger and there appeared to be a short bluff-like embankment where the water had cut away a portion of the hillside. He reached that, pulled himself up onto it and burrowed down into the grass and dry leaves. With luck the cavalrymen would ride on by without noticing. It was a slim chance, he knew, but it was safer than staying out in front and allowing Denning and the others to ride him down.

He saw the Yankee lieutenant then. The officer had flung out his men, was advancing slowly and carefully through the brush in a wide line, like men foraging for game. He was following the exact procedure Mosby had expected him to. The Ranger's eyes shifted. He picked up the rider nearest him. Hope lifted. The cavalryman was lagging behind Denning and the others, his horse moving with some difficulty through the more tangled edge of the brush. He would pass below the embankment, directly in front of Mosby. The Ranger watched the man narrowly. If he fell another yard or so behind . . .

Mosby drew his revolver, careful not to rustle

the dry leaves that surrounded him. He took the weapon by the barrel. Cautiously he drew his legs up beneath him, preparing himself to spring. It must be done as silently as possible, but speed would be the primary consideration; some of the other cavalrymen were bound to hear the commotion.

The soldier was immediately in front of him, six feet away and an arm's length below. Mosby took a deep breath and launched himself from the bluff. He came down behind the Yankee, astraddle the horse. As the startled animal bolted forward, Mosby brought his revolver sharply against the man's skull. The cavalryman groaned and sagged.

Mosby shoved him off the horse and sent him crashing into the brush. He seized the reins, jerked the horse savagely around. A yell went up from the rider next in line. Mosby fired at him at close range, saw him jolt and buckle. The Ranger pulled himself onto the saddle as the horse began to plunge wildly away into the maze of shrubbery.

Gunshots broke out, the bullets clipping through the leaves, thudding solidly into the trees. He was having a bad time of it with the frightened horse, pounding at breakneck speed over the uncertain footing along the creek. The animal, the whites of his eyes rolled back, was swerving from side to side, leaping fallen logs, shying and dodging as those possessed by some demon.

Mosby hung on grimly, allowed him to have the bit. If he didn't fall or crash into some obstacle, he would quickly outdistance Denning and his men. They came to the creek, dashed into it. The water seemed to slow the horse slightly and the Ranger began to get him under some semblance of control.

They broke out into the open and again the long legs of the horse lengthened out. Mosby heard more gunshots. He frowned. They had not come from the rear where he expected them — but from ahead. He crouched lower on his mount, both pistols out now and ready. If he were running head on into more Yankees, they were due for a taste of Confederate lead before they brought him down.

The horse began to slow and Mosby veered him back toward the creek with its sheltering growth. Denning and his men would come into view shortly and if he were not in sight he could gain a few moments by the confusion such would cause. He raced along through the narrow grove for another two hundred yards, again laced back across the stream. A fresh spatter of gunshots broke out up ahead. He threw an anxious look toward the crest of the hill, alarm rising within him.

Lovan, a lone horseman in the distance, was pounding for the top of the slope beyond. Hard behind him were the two cavalrymen Denning had assigned to the chase. Closing in from two other sides were more Yankees.

Chapter Nineteen

Hob Lovan would never make it.

That conviction strengthened in John Mosby's mind as he watched the soldiers narrow the gap that separated them from the fleeing scout. With their fresher horses they would soon overtake him, either capture or shoot him from the saddle.

The meaning was clear to the Ranger chief. No longer could he assume the scout would get Lee's message through to General Breckinridge. It was back in his hands again, and his plans for making it possible for Lovan to complete the mission were useless.

He raced along the fringe of brush for another hundred yards, striving to determine the best course he should now follow. The cavalrymen on Lovan's trail had not noticed him as yet and he had nothing to fear from them. But Denning and Neill, with their patrol, would soon make an appearance and once more be after him in full cry. Could he outrun them across the open ground? Could he stay out of musket range? Those were towering questions — and of vital importance.

He could only try.

He swung abruptly from the brush, struck out across the cleared ground for the slope lifting gently from the valley floor five hundred yards distant. Almost immediately he heard shouts behind him. Muskets and pistols began to crackle. Denning and his party had seen him.

But he had a fair lead, one that precluded accurate marksmanship and he paid no attention to the firing when he noted its shortcomings. He reached the foot of the hill and began the long climb. His horse was running easily, in much better condition than the luckless bay that had been shot out from under him at the Yankee camp. He was grateful for that now and it would have been better if Hob, too, had been forced to get another mount. As it was, the black he was riding was no match for the fresher horses of the army.

He could see nothing of Lovan and the cavalry that followed him. They were beyond the crest of the hill. He could hear an occasional burst of shooting coming from the grove over to his left. They had not brought down the old scout as yet, he thought with grim satisfaction.

He looked ahead. The ridge was only a hundred yards away. Behind him Neill and Denning, well out in front of the patrol, were coming up the grade. He had maintained his lead on the Yankees so far and now, if the country beyond the ridge offered any sort of cover at all, he should be able to shake them.

But the land rolled away in long, smooth dips.

Mosby swore softly to himself, settled lower on the saddle as he prepared for a race for his life. He could see a dark smudge of green on the far side, a full two miles or so distant. A grove of trees, a band of brush. He could not tell which — and it did not matter. To him it simply meant safety and escape. Whether he would make it or not was the question. On a strange horse, one whose qualities were unknown to him, he could only hope.

Denning and the Yankees began shooting again when they topped the ridge and raced down the opposite slope. They were only satisfying themselves that he was still beyond range, the Ranger realized. He had nothing to fear — yet.

He wondered again about Hob Lovan as he skimmed swiftly over the smooth ground on the long, seemingly tireless legs of his horse. If the scout managed to escape the vengeful soldiers it would be a miracle. He had heard no more gunshots coming from the area where he had last seen Lovan — but the meaning of that could be taken either way. Hob could still be fleeing — or he could be dead.

A deep sadness enveloped John Mosby suddenly. First Jeb Stuart, and now Lovan. Another close and loved friend. The loss of any Ranger was always a blow to him since he knew each personally, but there were those who were closer because of previous acquaintanceship. Thus it was with Hob. He shook his head slowly. It would be hard to think of the Rangers without Lovan as a part of them.

He glanced over his shoulder. He was maintaining his lead on the Yankees. The chase had settled down to a dogged, stubborn pursuit with neither party gaining or losing ground. It would be different, though, when he reached the grove. It was not far ahead now.

He risked another look at Denning and his men when he came to the first outcrop of brush. He was startled to see Neill and two of the cavalrymen had pulled well out in front of the others and had shortened the gap that separated him from the Yankees. They had realized the possibility of his escaping, once inside the trees, and with the three fastest horses in the patrol, were taking means to prevent it.

He rode into the wood and began pressing his mount for greater speed. But the grove was heavily overgrown and he lost time rapidly. He swerved to the right, headed north, away from his ultimate destination which lay to the west. He heard Neill and the cavalrymen enter, saw they had been close enough behind to note his change in course and were correcting accordingly.

They were pulling up fast. That they had stronger horses was apparent, and this set up a stream of worry within John Mosby. He again pressed his mount for a better pace, felt no response. He angled off in a new direction, once more doubling back toward the west. Neill and the Yankees followed. He was now in danger of encountering Denning and the remainder of the patrol. They should be somewhere within the grove by that moment. He must watch sharp and not become trapped between the two groups. Again he swung left. Instantly a yell went up. A musket cracked through the stillness of the forest.

In maneuvering, he had crossed in front of Neill! He pulled his horse up cruelly, almost bringing the animal to its haunches. They came about in a tight circle and plunged away through the brush. Two more gunshots rang out and Mosby heard the familiar moaning of the bullets as they passed near his head.

He drove straight on, dodging in and out of the trees, the low bushes, the clumps of tall shrubbery. He had no idea of what lay ahead; he could only hope the grove, with its protective cover, did not play out. If the Yankees pushed him into the open — he was done for.

He could not plan on darkness to mask his movements. It was still hours until nightfall, and it took only a brief fragment of time for a musket ball to catch up with a man to do its work. But he must not give up; he must not get careless and allow such to happen. He was the sole means now for getting Lee's orders through to Breckinridge. He had to make it.

He looked over his shoulder, feeling the hard grip of desperation settle over him. He could not see Neill and the men with him but he could still hear them as they crashed through the brush a hundred yards back, or possibly even less. He was steadily losing ground.

And running out of cover.

He saw the open ground through the thinning trees ahead. His heart sank but he raced on, hoping against hope that some means for salvation would present itself before it was too late.

He reached the end of the trees, spurted into a cleared field, and immediately veered right. He ducked back into the fringe of brush, taking advantage of every bit of concealment he could. He swept down into a shallow, broad ravine, hammered up the far side, broke out again into open ground.

His eyes, reaching ahead as they sought safety, caught a glimpse of houses at the far end of the field. A village. It instantly offered possibilities, an answer to his critical predicament. And then the sober realization that it, too, as Hazelville, could be in the hands of the Union army, chilled his hopes.

He would have to gamble on it. Crouched low over the taut neck of his striving mount, he rushed toward the settlement. He heard Neill and his men break into the field, yell, and swing on in his wake. They would remain in the open where their horses would find the going easier — and faster. This would shorten the distance that separated him from the Yankees since he must keep dodging in and out of the brush to prevent himself from becoming a target for their muskets and pistols.

The village, seemingly deserted in the afternoon sunlight, drew nearer. He could see no sign of soldiers and once again his spirits rose. If he could reach the scatter of houses and buildings, he had a chance; a slim one to be sure, but still a chance.

He drew abreast of the first structure, a weatherbeaten, sagging building that appeared to be the general store. He came to decision quickly. He would have to risk the possibility of soldiers being in the town, whether he wished to or not. Neill and the others were too close upon him to do anything else. And somewhere farther back would be Denning and the balance of the patrol. They would be catching up soon.

He swung into a narrow passageway that lay between the store and the building adjacent, raced down its length and burst into the wide street at the opposite end. He cut right, thundered along it, catching fleeting glimpses of startled faces watching from several windows and doors.

Near the end of the roadway he cut off, slicing between two houses, and doubled back. He saw a barn behind the third residence, its wide, double doors standing open. Without hesitation, he swerved into it.

He pulled the heaving horse to a sliding halt and leaped from the saddle. Hazing the nearly exhausted animal into a back stall, he turned, hurried to the building's entrance. Neill and his men were still in the street, the pound of their horses's hooves a hollow beating in the strange quiet.

The thudding ceased. Neill had reached the end of the roadway and halted. Mosby waited, endeavored to figure what the big sergeant would do next. Wait for Denning, he guessed, and then begin a house-to-house search of the town.

He heard more horses then. That would be the Yankee lieutenant arriving with the remainder of the patrol. The Ranger watched from the doorway, his eyes on that portion of the street visible between two houses that stood in front of the barn. He saw Denning and his blue-uniformed men ride by slowly to rejoin Neil.

Mosby considered the advisability of mounting his horse and riding out of the village at its far end while the Yankees gathered in the street. He discarded the idea; the town was surrounded by open country. He would be noticed almost im-

mediately — and he doubted if his mount was up
to making another fast sprint without a little rest.

But to remain there in the barn would be inviting
discovery.

He concluded his best hopes lay outside. Once
they located him within the building he would be
trapped, and the prospects of fighting his way
through a half dozen heavily armed Yankees
singlehanded would be poor. He turned then, took
up the reins of his spent horse and led him around
to the rear of the barn. There he tied him securely
and returned to the front of the building where he
took up a stand at the corner.

He did not have long to wait. Almost at once two
cavalrymen, on foot, came around the rear of the
end house. They were checking the backs of the
homes, the barns and sheds that stood behind
them. Other men would be moving down the street
and along the hind sides of the houses on the opposite row of the street.

He watched the two blue-coated men approach.
They were doing a thorough job, looking into
every structure regardless of size, and maintaining
a close watch on the houses as well.

The pair drew nearer. Mosby could hear their
voices but he could not make out the words.
Something pertaining to Neill, it seemed. It appeared they had small use for the big sergeant.
Mosby drew back as they halted in the doorway to
the barn.

"Go ahead. I'll stand watch here," one said, his
voice plain now.

The other, pushing his forage cap to the back of
his head, drew his pistol. He leaned forward,
peered into the shadowy interior of the building.

"Ain't no horse in there," he said. "Was he hidin' inside, there'd be a horse."

"Better go on in and have a look anyway. You recollect what the sergeant said."

The Yankee nodded and slowly entered the barn. Mosby listened to his cautious movements. When the sounds began to fade and he knew the man was returning to his companion, he turned, dropped silently back to the rear of the structure where his horse waited.

He untied the animal, led him around to the opposite side of the barn and again stopped. He anchored the horse to a clump of brush and made his way to the front. The Yankees had gone on to the next shed.

Mosby hurried to his horse and stepped to the saddle. Now, by keeping the barn's sprawling bulk between himself and the soldiers, and heading straight out from the village, he should be able to escape unnoticed.

He walked the horse softly over the uneven ground, past two or three small sheds and outbuildings. He came to the last house, his body tense, his nerves taut as fiddle strings. If no soldiers remained in the street, if all were, as he thought, searching through the town, he would have a clear road.

But it was not to be so easy.

A figure stepped suddenly from the corner of the house. A big, red-faced, thick-shouldered man whose arm came up in a swift blur. In his hand he held a cocked revolver.

Sergeant Amos Neill.

Chapter Twenty

John Mosby knew he was looking at death.

There was the pure shine of hatred in the sergeant's eyes, the determination to kill in the tense, angry way he crouched. The Confederate leader threw himself to one side, clawed at the pistol at his hip.

"Halt — you damn guerrilla . . ." Neill yelled and fired.

Stinging particles of wood and leather peppered Mosby's face and neck. The bullet had struck the pommel of the saddle, shattered a corner of it. Mosby threw a hasty, answering shot, but he was leaning far over and his aim was poor. It was a clean miss.

As his horse shied away the Ranger could see Jasper Denning at the opposite end of the town. The lieutenant was coming toward them at a run. Other Yankee cavalrymen, attracted by the gunshots, were rushing into the street. Mosby thumbed back the hammer of his revolver, struggled to control his horse, got set for a shot.

He saw Neill's weapon blossom smoke again,

and knew instantly the horse was hit. The animal faltered, his legs gave out suddenly. He went to his knees. Mosby, out of the saddle fast, threw himself to the side. To get caught beneath the thrashing animal would be fatal. He struck the ground just as the horse went into a wild spasm of kicking, and rolled free. A cool desperateness was upon the Ranger now; he knew his life hung in the balance. What happened in the next few seconds of time would determine whether he lived or died.

He saw the triumphant look spread across Neill's flushed face as he swung his pistol up for the kill. Mosby took careful aim, ignoring the surging urgency that lashed at his nerves. He squeezed off his shot. The ball caught the big sergeant in the breast, drove him backwards a half dozen steps. He fired again as Neill brought his revolver up once more. The soldier went down.

Shouts were rising in the street. Muskets began to snap. Denning was yelling to his men to close in, to rush, to shoot. Mosby wheeled away from his dead mount, eyes searching for an escape. He saw the cavalrymen's horses tied to a hitch rail alongside the store building just beyond Neill. He did not hesitate, raced across to them, drawing his second, fully loaded pistol as he ran. He sent a final shot whistling down the street at the Yankees when he reached the corner of the building and sprinted to the waiting horses. He jerked free the reins of the nearest, a tall sorrel, and leaped onto the saddle. He paused long enough to release the remaining horses, sent them galloping off.

He rode in behind them, drove them before him a short distance until they began to scatter. He forgot them then and concentrated on reaching the distant green band that was a grove of trees. Tension was running out of him now and he was feeling easier. Denning and his Yankee cavalrymen would give up after this. With Neill dead, their horses scattered, there was little possibility of their preventing him from reaching New Market.

The horse he had taken, more by accident than from choice, was a fine animal. He ran smoothly and with no show of effort, covering the ground in long strides that ate up the miles rapidly.

When he reached the trees Mosby looked back toward the village. He could barely make out the Yankees, no more than dark figures at the end of the street. There was one horse visible. Likely it had been borrowed from one of the townsmen for use in rounding up their straying mounts.

He rode on through the grove, now taking a direct line for the west. He could not be too far from Thornton's Gap, he reasoned, and with a faint hope beginning to stir in him, decided to wait there until sundown on the chance that Hob Lovan had escaped and would put in an appearance.

He could not reconcile himself to accepting the fact of the scout's death. Lovan had been with him since the start of the war and together they had lived through many desperate and seemingly hopeless encounters with the Yankees. Hob Lovan was the sort of man that couldn't be killed — but he had felt that way about Jeb Stuart, too; and Stuart was now buried.

He reached Massanutten Mountain and halted a short distance below the pass shortly before sundown. He drew off into the deep brush, tied the sorrel to a tree and made a swift scouting excursion of the area. There were no signs of Lovan. He withdrew then to a point where he could observe anyone approaching and remained there until full dark.

Finally, with heavy heart, he concluded there was no reason to delay longer. Hob Lovan was not coming — he would never come. The worst had occurred. Mosby walked slowly to his horse and climbed wearily to the saddle.

Near the summit of the mountain he heard riders on the western side and wheeled off into the darkness to let them pass. They were not soldiers, he saw when they drew abreast, but farmers. He allowed them to go by without interruption, and when he could no longer hear them he resumed his journey.

He would be getting Lee's message to John Breckinridge well ahead of time, despite all the delays. He had not expected to reach the Confederate general until that next morning. Now he would be there a good eight hours ahead of schedule. That would be of importance to Lee's plans. Breckinridge could move out at dawn with his division, and his men, bolstered by the men freed at Hazelville and those Keswick hoped to escape with from Grant's camp, would reinforce the Confederate army immeasurably.

He descended the western slope of the mountain at a trot, taking no pains to avoid the well-traveled road. At the bottom he took the left-hand fork and after a time, he began to see the lights of New Market. He had no idea of where Breckinridge would be camped other than being told by Lee that the officer would be somewhere close to the settlement. The natural location would be on the southern outskirts where there was ample level ground, someone else had informed him.

It was strange that he saw no watch fires, and it disturbed John Mosby considerably. It seemed also that there should be lanterns visible by that time. There was nothing, only the lamps glowing yellow through the windows of the homes.

He pulled to a halt at the first house to which he came along the road. It stood at the extreme edge of the town. Dismounting, he moved in close, always cautious, and paused at a window. Keeping back, he peered in. A man and woman, with two small children, were seated about a table. The man, a lean, black-bearded individual with a large nose and wide forehead, was reading from a book.

Mosby studied the room. The lamp in the center of the table did not reach into the dark corners and he could not determine what lay there but it looked safe enough. He walked to the door, rapped lightly. He heard a chair scrape across the bare floor and then the panel swung inward. The man stared at him.

"What is it?"

Mosby said, "I'm looking for General Breckinridge. I'm told he's camped around here. Can you tell me where?"

The farmer continued to study the Ranger. Then, shrugging his shoulders, he said, "Breckinridge is gone. Pulled out yesterday."

Chapter Twenty-One

Disappointment and weariness slogged through John Mosby. He placed a hand against the wall of the house, leaned heavily upon it.

"Where to?"

The farmer shook his head. It was plain he was fencing. Uncertain whether Mosby was friend or foe, he was taking no chances by saying too much. Similar precautions were moving through the Ranger's mind.

"Was a devil of a fight here yesterday morning," the man said. "Breckinridge and Sigel. Union army finally gave way and retreated. Breckinridge went after them."

"Which way."

"Across the river. Sigel burned the bridge but that didn't stop the Confederates!"

There was a faint ring of pride in the man's tone. Mosby decided to gamble. "I'm from General Lee's headquarters. Important that I find Breckinridge."

The farmer leaned forward, looked more closely

at the Ranger. He drew back suddenly. "Hey, now! You wouldn't be John Mosby, would you?"

"I am."

The farmer stepped back out of the door. "Come in, come in, Major! Didn't recognize you with that beard you're growing. My name's Colmor. Come in and set for a minute — have a bite to eat. Look like you could use it."

Mosby hesitated. He should be on his way. John Breckinridge must be found and Lee's orders delivered. But to sit down, to relax for a few minutes, to have a cup of hot tea or coffee and perhaps a mouthful of food, would be welcome. And he needed more details on Breckinridge.

"Thank you, Mr. Colmor," he said in his calm, polite way and moved by the farmer into the house.

Colmor's wife nodded to him as he entered and then took the children into a back room. The farmer waved the Ranger into one of the chairs at the table, turned to the stove.

"Make yourself comfortable, Major. Take me just a minute to get you a plate of vittles. Got coffee, too. Weak but good."

Mosby sank gratefully into the chair. He glanced around the simply but comfortably furnished room. The war, with all its terrible death and destruction, seemed far removed from that quiet house. Neat, orderly, showing the touch of a woman's hand, it made him think of his own home, his wife and children, and the long, hungry loneliness he knew so well possessed him once more.

Things would be beautiful around the family place now. Flowers, set out and so carefully cultivated by his wife, would be blooming. The fields would be green and the trees fully clothed. The garden would be planted and the livestock — three cows, a half dozen hogs, a mixed flock of chickens, ducks and gabbling geese — if they had not fallen victims to the war's demands would be wandering about the barn and the yard that fronted it. It would be wonderful to be home again and he, too, like Tom Scott and the Confederate colonel at Hazelville, and thousands of others, could wish the war were over and he could return to the life he loved.

But there was little hope of that day coming soon. He glanced at the book Colmor had been reading. It was the Bible and it lay open on the table. The marker had been placed at the twentieth Psalm; *The Lord hear thee in the day of trouble.* The war touched all, he thought. Some more than others. But in the end all would benefit for from the mighty struggle, a stronger and better country would be born.

"Here you are, Major," Colmor said, moving up to the table. He held a plate of boiled meat and cornbread in one hand, a cup of steaming, black coffee in the other. "It ain't much but then we don't have a lot these days."

Mosby accepted the food and drink gratefully. He began to eat at once, not realizing how hungry he had been. And the coffee, made from grounds used over and over again, was nevertheless excellent.

Colmor sat down across from him, remained silent while the Ranger ate. When Mosby was finished he took up the plate and cup, returned it to the kitchen.

"Not a drop of liquor in the house or we'd have

a drink to top that off with," he said, coming back and sitting down. "No tobacco for a smoke, either."

"It's all right," Mosby replied. "I appreciate the meal. What happened around here?"

"Well, Sigel had been hanging around for some time. Same with General Breckinridge. Early yesterday morning they started having an artillery duel, shot at each other across the town. Breckinridge had come up from the south side. Went at it hot and heavy.

"The Yankees started falling back about noon when some of the cadets from the Military Institute managed to take over one of Sigel's batteries. About fifty of the boys got killed but it broke Sigel's back and by dark he was on the run. He crossed the river and headed north with Breckinridge after him."

"Confederate losses pretty high?"

"Not too bad, except for the cadets. Most of the wounded are down in town being looked after by the womenfolk. How're things going for General Lee?"

"He's holding Grant but needs support. That's why I have to find Breckinridge."

"Expect he'll be somewheres between here and Cedar Creek. Never heard much shooting during the day. Guess the Yankees ain't stopping to fight."

Mosby rose to his feet. "I'm obliged to you for the hospitality. Expect I'd better move on . . ."

"You're welcome to spend the night," Colmor broke in. "From the looks of you I'd say you'd come a far piece without much rest."

"You're right, but it's important that I reach Breckinridge."

"I understand. Just turn around and head back the way you come. That'll be north. Stay on this side of the mountain. You'll run into him up there somewhere."

The Ranger nodded his thanks, walked toward the door. "Like to say again how much I . . ."

He paused, the faint drumming of oncoming horses catching his attention. Colmor spun, blew out the lamp. Together they moved to the window, glanced out into the night.

"Two men," the farmer murmured. "Must have rode down from the mountain."

Mosby watched the horsemen pull to a stop in front of Colmor's place. He was glad he had left the sorrel off in the brush. They had not noticed him.

"Yankees," Colmor said. "Sure as the devil! Now what are they doing back here?"

Mosby looked more closely. His shoulders sagged as he recognized one of the pair. "The officer's name is Denning," he said in an exhausted voice. "He's been on my trail ever since I left Lee's camp."

Chapter Twenty-Two

Denning and one cavalryman. Mosby studied them from the edge of the window. Where were the others? There should be at least two more.

He had the answer a moment later. The missing pair, leading the sorrel, rode out of the shadows, halted behind the Yankee lieutenant.

"They found your horse, Major," Colmor said in a useless statement of what the Ranger could see.

"There a back way out of this house?" Mosby asked, his mind and reflexes performing normally again.

"Sure. But how you going to get far on foot?"

Mosby shook his head. "I don't know, but I can't stay here. They'll be knocking on your door in a minute or two."

"If I had a horse you could take him . . ."

"Don't worry about it. I'll find a way. How do I get out of here?"

"Follow me," Colmor said, suddenly filled with the urgency of the moment. He wheeled, led Mosby through the next room where the woman and children lay sleeping, out onto a back porch.

"Walk straight ahead," the farmer whispered. "They'll not see you. Cut left when you get to that patch of fruit trees, and keep going. You'll be headed in the right direction."

Mosby nodded. "How about you? Will you be all right?"

"Sure. I've handled Yankees before. Good luck."

"Good luck," Mosby echoed and slipped off into the darkness of the yard.

He gained the small stand of trees, halted. He disliked the thought of leaving Colmor to face Denning and the Yankee cavalrymen alone. The farmer had befriended him, was a Southern sympathizer and could conceivably come to grief if Denning decided he was an enemy of the Union. But Colmor seemed unafraid — and the matter of getting Lee's message to Breckinridge was still the paramount issue.

He moved on, following Colmor's instructions. He had no idea of how far he must travel to overtake the force; Colmore did not know if Breckinridge was in pursuit of Sigel or had simply driven him up the valley for some distance and halted. It was of no consequence; Breckinridge must be found even if it meant hiking all the way to Maryland.

He came to the bridge, a charred, ghostly mass of blackened timbers but repaired to the extent that it could be crossed on foot. With the mountain to his right hand and keeping well off the road, he struck a course up the valley. He must be alert for Denning, he knew. The Yankee lieutenant, as soon as he was satisfied the man he sought was no longer around Colmor's, would resume the chase. And since he, too, would know the direction Breckinridge had taken, he likewise would head up the valley.

Mosby alternated his pace between a walk and a trot. It was a comfortable night, one he would have enjoyed were he not so weary and his problems so pressing. There had been very little time for rest, he reflected, since Spottsylvania; but rest would come later, after he caught up with Breckinridge.

Shortly after midnight he heard horses on the road. He drew off into the brush and waited. There were four riders and one glance told him it was Jasper Denning and the remnants of his Yankee cavalry patrol. They were riding slowly, evidently not too certain of their ground but still determined to locate and stop him before he could complete his mission.

Likely they were at a loss as to where they should begin a search. They knew he had left Colmor's on foot, since they had recovered the horse he had taken. Now they would not know if he had obtained another elsewhere, or was proceeding without one. Denning would be upset, at loose ends as to what he should do.

They were a long time showing up, Mosby noted. Apparently Colmor had delayed them in one manner or another, giving Mosby as much leeway as possible. He hoped the farmer had not suffered at the hands of the Yankees — but Colmor looked to be a man who could take care of himself.

He waited until the four horsemen were out of hearing and then resumed the trail. He must be doubly careful now; the Yankees were between him and Breckinridge, and Denning, conceivably, would ride a considerable distance ahead, to a point where he knew Mosby could not have reached, and there throw a cordon across the valley with the idea in mind of intercepting the Ranger. He should be on the alert for just such a maneuver.

He pushed on, walking, running, walking, running in a monotonous but mile-covering pace. He moved mechanically, so weary he scarcely knew when his brain ordered the changes. His reflexes were automatic and he did things without conscious knowledge.

When the first streaks of gray began to brighten the east, he gradually became more alert although the weights that dragged at his body lessened none. He looked ahead through the trees. He was approaching a long ridge, he saw, and beyond it he thought he detected several wisps of smoke. This heartened him and he quickened his step. But he kept to the brush, always aware of the need for caution.

He was thankful for that inbred wariness. As he neared the crest of the hogback, he caught sight of Denning and his three cavalrymen. They had halted, dismounted, and stood looking down into what apparently was a valley.

He worked his way around them, giving them a wide berth, and crossed the ridge a good quarter mile to the left of where they had positioned themselves. A sigh of relief slipped through him when he beheld Breckinridge's camp spread out below. He had finally caught up with the Confederate general and his command.

He lay spread-eagled along the rim and studied the encampment. Watch fires still winked in the half dark and he could see a few soldiers moving about. He realized he should continue, that he must reach the camp before full daylight fell across the land or Denning and his men could still prevent him from reaching his goal. And if he allowed the Yankees to trap him on the ridge, he would be forced to watch Breckinridge march out and Lee's order would be delayed another twelve or fourteen hours, perhaps longer.

He fell to studying the encampment. The main body of it was a thousand yards away, in the center of the valley. From the ridge to a distance half way down the slope there was a scattering of brush and trees. There followed this open ground for another two hundred yards or so and then came more bush. Just beyond that the camp began, a row of tents, several small fires and sleeping soldiers lying rolled in their blankets.

He could make it to the edge of the brush without drawing Denning's attention. From there it would be a serious problem. He considered for a few moments and then moved on. He gained nothing by remaining still and he should take advantage of what little darkness still held. He slipped quietly down the slope, careful to dislodge no loose gravel or rocks and avoiding contact with the brush that might set up a noise audible to the Yankees. He came to the last of the cover and halted.

Daylight was coming swiftly, once begun, and he saw his hopes of racing across the cleared ground undetected by Denning, fading with each succeeding moment. Crouched in the brush he looked back up the slope. He could see only the heads of the Yankees. They were taking care not to be observed by the camp.

He knew then what he must do — make a break for it. He could not remain idle, caught half way between the Yankees and Breckinridge. He drew his two pistols, checked their cylinders. They were fully loaded and ready. Taking one in each hand, he paused while he took several deep breaths. Then, leaping to his feet he started at a run for the next stand of screening cover a long two hundred yards away.

Before he had covered a quarter of the distance he heard the Yankees. They had seen him bolt from his hiding place and sprint into the open. Immediately they had taken to their horses and now were plunging down the slope at reckless speed. That they would encounter no opposition from the sleeping camp was most probable; and the pickets would be too distant to do them any harm.

Half way John Mosby risked a glance at the slope. The Yankees were almost upon him. They were holding their fire, unwilling to arouse the camp, he realized. Instantly he opened up with his left-hand gun, sending three rapid reports echoing across the valley. The bullets fell short, as he expected they would, but now, if any sentries were nearby, they would be on the alert.

Denning and his men began to shoot then. The Ranger started to weave back and forth, offering no easy target. He fired a fourth shot but the Yankees came on. He heard the whirr of a musket ball, knew from that they were now in effective range, and that if he survived their concerted fire he would indeed be fortunate. He looked ahead desperately. Fifty yards . . . He put all his strength into a final burst of speed. The Yankees were so near he could hear the squeaking of saddle leather above the thunder of their horses' hooves. He twisted about, determined to make his bullets count, tried to take aim. Running hard as he was, it was impossible. He gave it up, snapped a shot at the nearest cavalryman.

He caught a glimpse of Jasper Denning's tight, grim face. The Yankee lieutenant was a man with plenty of nerve, there was no doubting that. To move in so close to an entire Confederate army took courage; but he had a job to do, too, as Mosby, and he was determined to accomplish it.

He saw Denning level his pistol, try to bring it to bear. He jerked to one side, caused the officer to miss. One of the cavalrymen surged in close, steadying his musket across a crooked forearm. Mosby tried to veer in stride, to run faster but the strength was not in him. His lungs were screaming and felt as though they would burst. And then suddenly two shots rang out from the depths of the brush just ahead. Mosby's heart leaped. Confederate sentries! They had waited until Denning and his Yankees were near enough for a certain shot.

Mosby heard one of the Yankees yell in pain. There was a hard pound of horses, a flurry of shooting but the bullets were beyond him. He reached the outcrop of brush, staggered and fell. He rolled, looked back toward the ridge. Denning and one man were pounding hard for the summit. The two remaining cavalrymen lay sprawled on the grass a dozen yards away.

Mosby struggled to his feet, still heaving for breath. He grinned tightly at the young corporal who came running up.

"I'm Major John Mosby. I'm obliged to you — now get me to General Breckinridge fast as you can."

Chapter Twenty-Three

An hour later John Mosby stood with Breckinridge before the officer's tent. The order had been given. The entire army would reverse itself and begin a forced march for Richmond. General Imboden had been instructed to throw out his cavalry at once, form an advance guard as well as protect the flanks and rear lines. They would reach Lee in time, the square-jawed, clean-shaven Breckinridge assured Mosby.

"Only one thing that bothers me," he added. "Leaves this whole valley up to Grumble Jones to patrol. And all he's got is a thousand men, most of them old and with little or no equipment. And of course the cadets from the Military Academy — God bless 'em! But then, that's no problem of yours. You're due some rest. I'll order a bed prepared for you in one of the supply wagons. You can catch up on your sleep while we travel."

"Not necessary," Mosby replied. "Just give me a horse. I'll do my napping in the saddle, something I'm accustomed to."

Breckinridge smiled. "Whatever you say, Major. Well, what have we here? Prisoners?"

The Ranger swung about. His eyes flared with surprise. Two Yankees — Jasper Denning and the last member of his cavalry patrol — hands above their heads, were moving up under the leveled muskets of a sentry and a tattered, disheveled old man with a stained bandage about his leg.

Hob Lovan!

A shout exploded involuntarily from John Mosby's lips. He rushed by the glowering Yankees, threw his arms around the slight body of the scout.

"I thought they'd got you!" he exclaimed, his voice oddly hoarse.

Lovan grinned and spat. "Well, they come mighty close, Major. Was quite a chore shakin' off all them bluebellies but I finally done it. But I'm sure glad to see you. Was worryin' me no end, 'specially when you didn't show at Thornton's Gap."

"I waited there until after dark," Mosby replied. "Then went on. Figured you couldn't make it."

"Was late. About midnight when I rode up. Then I come on here. Was just climbin' to the top of the ridge when I heard shootin'. Then I seen these two varmints a-high-tailin' it for tall timber. Wasn't much I could do but step out and take them prisoner. You all right?"

John Mosby looked at the scout and smiled. "Never was better," he said. "Let's hunt up the surgeon and get that leg of yours fixed proper. We've got to get back to Richmond."

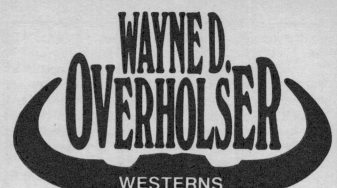

WAYNE D. OVERHOLSER

WESTERNS

FREE!!
BOOKS BY MAIL
CATALOGUE

BOOKS BY MAIL will share with you our current bestselling books as well as hard to find specialty titles in areas that will match your interests. You will be updated on what's new in books at no cost to you. Just fill in the coupon below and discover the convenience of having books delivered to your home.

PLEASE ADD $1.00 TO COVER THE COST OF POSTAGE & HANDLING.

BOOKS BY MAIL

320 Steelcase Road E.,
Markham, Ontario L3R 2M1

210 5th Ave., 7th Floor
New York, N.Y., 10010

Please send Books By Mail catalogue to:

Name _____
                    (please print)
Address _____

City _____

Prov./State _____ P.C./Zip _____

(BBM1)